SWEET DREAMS
BAKE SHOP

A SWEET COVE, MASSACHUSETTS COZY
MYSTERY BOOK 1

J. A. WHITING

To hear about new books and book sales, please sign up for my mailing list at:

www.jawhiting.com

❁ Created with Vellum

For my family, with love

1

Angie Roseland loved this time of morning when the streets and sidewalks were quiet, the air was fresh, and the daylight filtering through puffy white clouds was bright and new. The air was unusually warm for mid-April and the change in the weather lifted Angie's spirits. It had been a harsh winter and a wet spring, so a warm sunny day was especially welcome.

Angie had her shoulder-length, honey blonde hair piled on top of her head and held there with a clip. She adjusted the canvas bag on her shoulder as she bent to insert the key into the lock of the shop's blue door. Swinging it open, she flicked the switch to turn on the overhead lights of the cozy café.

The words "overhead lights" didn't really do justice when describing the lighting in Angie's bake shop. Those words conjured an image of harsh banks of fluorescent bulbs stuck inside of a plastic cover. Angie had spent many hours searching for just the right pieces to illuminate her small coffee and desserts shop. She wanted her bake shop to be a welcoming and comfortable spot for her patrons and she believed that lighting was an important aspect of creating a cozy café.

Two medium-sized cut glass, crystal, and pewter chandeliers hung from the ceiling, and the small pieces of glass and crystal caught the light of the bulbs and softly bounced the rays off of the ivory ceiling and the light mocha walls. The shimmering lights always made Angie happy when she arrived for work each early morning.

She hummed to herself as she tucked her purse under the counter and headed to the back room to put her lunch in the small fridge she kept to one side of the preparation area. Slipping a pale pink apron over her head and tying the back straps, Angie returned to the front room of the café, turned on classical music, prepared coffee pots, heated water for tea, checked the supplies in the cabinets, and started the process of baking her breads, muffins, and tea cakes.

The door opened causing a little bell to tinkle.

"Hey, sis," Courtney called to her older sister. "What's cookin'?"

Angie looked up and smiled. "Ha. You need to come up with a new line." She went to the bank of windows and opened one of them wide. Because of the long, freezing winter and the cool, wet spring, the windows hadn't been open in months. "It's like an early summer day. Let's let in the fresh air."

Twenty-one-year-old Courtney helped open two of the front windows, and then she headed to the back room to get her apron. She was a senior at a Boston university and she often returned to the town of Sweet Cove on weekends to help out at the bake shop. She called out from the back room. "You're very cheerful for someone who is about to get kicked out of her shop."

Angie sighed. "I'm just trying to enjoy my last few weeks here." She moved to the work station and made two vanilla lattes. Courtney returned to the front room wearing her apron and accepted one of the lattes from Angie.

"Any news on your search for a new space?" Courtney took a small sip from her white cup.

Angie shook her head and frowned. "Any place that's available, I can't afford and anything I can afford isn't available. The real estate agent is looking and listening for any possibilities, but it looks like I'm not going to be open anywhere in this town this summer."

Angie had opened her Sweet Dreams Bake Shop in Sweet Cove, Massachusetts only a year ago. Now the building was being sold and the new owners had different plans and weren't renewing Angie's lease.

Sweet Cove was a perfect small town right on the Atlantic Ocean tucked on the North Shore only thirty minutes from Boston. A train station on the edge of town received several trains a day from the city and when the weather was good they carried droves of day-trippers to Sweet Cove. There were a number of bed and breakfasts, small inns, and quaint hotels, along with a variety of shops that lined the cozy streets selling books, jewelry, clothes, ice cream, and anything else anybody might need or want.

The town had an old-fashioned movie theatre, pharmacy, and small grocery store. Angie, her sisters, and mom had vacationed in Sweet Cove for years, and some of her ancestors, including her grandmother, had lived in the town all of their lives.

Angie had been searching for a place to start her café business and was thrilled when the small space in Sweet Cove came up for rent last year. The shop was doing well and Angie built a loyal following of regular customers drawn from the permanent residents in the area, in addition to the tourists who frequented her café. Now that she wouldn't be able to stay in town, she would have to start from scratch wherever she ended up moving. Despite her heavy heart, Angie couldn't spend time dwelling on her dilemma as the regulars would be arriving soon for their morning beverages and bakery treats.

The door opened and Angie's employee, Lisa Barrows, entered the café and greeted Angie and Courtney. Lisa was in her early sixties, divorced, and had recently moved to Sweet Cove after living in central Massachusetts for over forty years. Lisa had been born one town over from Sweet Cove and spent the first years of her life in the area. She was now retired from a teaching position and, having lost her mother last year, Lisa decided to return to the seacoast. She wanted to keep busy and was happy to find a job at the bake shop. She worked three full days and three half days. Lisa, with her stylish, short silver hair, was energetic and efficient, and Angie was happy to have her help.

The women chatted amiably as they hurried about the shop getting ready for the first customers of the day.

THE BAKE SHOP was in full swing with a line of customers waiting for their beverage orders. People stood in front of the bakery cases choosing treats for takeout and other customers were perched on the five counter stools sipping coffees and eating muffins and homemade donuts. The shop had ten café tables with four chairs around each one. Angie always had little glass vases filled with fresh flowers on the tables. All of the seats were taken by local residents who sat discussing the latest town news and gossip before heading out to their jobs or errands. The local real estate agent, Betty Hayes, a boisterous middle-aged woman who knew everything that was going on in Sweet Cove, was engaged in her daily schmoozing, always nosing around for a property to sell.

Angie was slightly annoyed with Betty because she didn't seem to be putting much effort into finding a new place for the cafe. Angie realized that her need for a new space for the bake shop was probably at the bottom of the real estate agent's priority list since finding a rental space wouldn't provide much of a commission.

The door opened and a small older woman with nearly white hair pulled into a loose bun, leaned on her cane, and stepped into the café. Angie caught her eye and waved to her. The woman beamed a lovely smile at Angie. Lisa hurried over, took the woman's arm and led her to a table that was opening up. "Good morning, Professor Linden. Here's a table right here. Would you like your usual?"

"Yes, Lisa, thank you. I'll wait for Angie to make it." A fleeting scowl passed over Lisa's face and then was gone. Professor Linden preferred that Angie make her first latte of the day. The professor took a seat at the small table near the window. A fresh breeze came through the screen and ruffled the petals of the flowers in the vase.

Courtney walked over to greet the professor. "Can I get you something to eat?"

"What did Angie bake today?" The professor would only eat the items that Angie baked. Some customers thought that Angie had a special talent for baking and they preferred to order the specialties that were prepared by her.

"She made almond cake, blueberry scones, and

the Russian teacake cookies," Courtney told the woman.

"I'd like a blueberry scone, please." The professor smiled and opened her newspaper.

Professor Linden, a town selectman for many years, had retired from teaching mathematics at a university in Boston and she'd lived in Sweet Cove off and on since she was a little girl. Her house, a huge eighteen-room Victorian, was on Beach Street just around the corner from the Sweet Dreams Bake Shop. The professor and her late husband purchased the house many years ago and even though Professor Linden admitted that the place was much too large for her, she'd decided that she would never sell it.

Courtney brought a mocha latte to the table with a napkin and a scone on a pale blue plate. "Here you are. Angie just made the latte for you. Enjoy."

The professor nibbled at her scone and sipped her drink as town residents stopped by her table to chat. A pleasant buzz of conversations filled the air of the café as people came and went. Betty, the real estate agent, joined the professor for several minutes and then some business people who were interested in building on some town wetlands stopped by to talk. Angie joked that it was like the professor held office hours every morning in the bake shop.

After she delivered some slices of banana bread and two coffees to the town's police chief and patrol officer, Angie noticed a lull at the professor's table, so she sat down with her for a few minutes.

"How's your hip, Professor?" Angie asked.

"It's a bit better. It gets sore after strolling here and back home again, but I think it's certainly improving." Professor Linden had a pacemaker and about a month ago she experienced a dizzy spell in the kitchen of her home, fell, and bruised her hip. Angie was walking past the house to deliver some muffins to one of the nearby restaurants when she heard the professor's cat howling inside. It was pretty clear that something was wrong from the caterwauling coming through the open window.

Angie investigated and ended up calling an ambulance for Professor Linden. The Sweet Cove weekly newspaper did a story praising the feline for sounding the alarm. Quite a few of the locals teased Angie that the cat had received more attention than she did for helping Professor Linden.

Angie chatted with the professor for a little while, discussing recipes and gardening and travel. "I will surely miss you when you have to close this café." The professor patted Angie's hand. "And I will certainly miss all of your delightful treats. There's something magical about them."

Angie's eyes sparkled at the professor's compliment. "Thank you, Professor. You've always been so encouraging ever since I set up shop here in town. It means a lot to me. I'll come back to Sweet Cove to visit," Angie told her. "And, I'll be sure to bring you a box of your favorite baked goods whenever I come to see you."

The professor frowned at the thought of Angie leaving. "It just won't be the same without you. I've grown quite fond of you, you know."

Angie nodded and her blue eyes got misty. "I'm going to miss you, too. But we still have four weeks before I have to close. We'll make the most of it." She forced a smile.

Just then the shop door opened and two men in suits stepped in.

"So this is what's on the other side of the wall." The taller man pointed towards the café's back room, and then he looked around the front space. "Who is running this shop?" His voice carried a tone of authority and he appeared to be someone who knew his way around a boardroom. He had blue eyes and dark brown hair showing some gray at the temples. He looked to be in his mid-forties. He glanced about looking for the person in charge of the café. Angie rose from her seat.

"I'm Angie Roseland."

"Davis Williams." He shifted his briefcase into his left hand and reached to shake with Angie.

The second man who entered the shop stepped from behind Davis Williams. He appeared to be in his early thirties, with sandy blonde hair and bright blue eyes. He was trim, and his suit was well-cut and fitted. He smiled, showing a perfect row of white teeth. "Josh Williams. Davis' brother." He extended his hand to Angie and she shook with him.

"Your shop is great," Josh said, looking around.

Angie wondered who these two men were and why they were looking for her.

The Professor placed her hands on the table in order to push herself up. She reached for her cane. "This shop is great. Maybe someday you'll be sorry you drove this young woman from Sweet Cove."

Angie looked with puzzled eyes from the professor to the men.

Courtney watched the exchange of words and realized the professor was leaving. She placed the professor's usual takeout cup of hazelnut latte into a paper bag and brought it over to her. The professor took the bag, nodded at Angie, shuffled to the exit and left the café, pulling the door shut with a bang.

"We're the building's new owners." Davis Williams said to Angie, unfazed by the older woman's reprimand.

"Oh." Angie couldn't help a frown forming on her face.

"We'd like to see the backroom, if we may. It would only take a minute. We're trying to iron out the details of the renovation plans." Davis adjusted the cuff of his suit.

Angie bristled inwardly even though she knew the two men had every right to make the request. She felt protective of her little shop and wished they would just go away.

"If it's not a good time," said Josh Williams, "we can come back later."

His brother shot him a look.

"Um," Angie said. "No. It's okay. Go ahead. Do what you have to do." She turned away from the men and started to clear away dishes from some of the tables.

Courtney stood near the entrance to the backroom with her arms crossed over her chest, her eyes shooting daggers at the two men. She scowled at the Williams' brothers as they walked past her.

"Courtney." Angie shook her head slightly indicating that her younger sister should just ignore the men. "Could you help me clear?"

After ten minutes, the men returned to the front of the café. "Thank you, Angie," Josh said. "Sorry to get in the way." He held Angie's eyes.

Josh's gaze caused an unexpected little zing to shoot through Angie's heart. She gave him a quick nod and turned to finish the frozen chocolate drink she was making.

The café was quieter now that the morning rush was over and the women worked to replenish the bakery case, run the dishwashers, and get ready for the second wave of customers who would start streaming in around noon.

Josh approached the counter and sat on one of the stools. "We drove up from Boston," he told Angie. "The traffic was terrible. I'd love to have a coffee and whatever you suggest to eat with it." He smiled at her and Angie almost blushed.

"Josh?" Davis Williams stood ram-rod straight at the door. He had a clipboard in one hand and his briefcase in the other. He wasn't planning on staying.

"I'll catch up with you," Josh said. "I need a coffee."

Davis scowled but didn't say anything. He had

things to accomplish and didn't want to sit around in a bake shop. Especially one he had plans to rip out of his newly acquired building. "Meet me at the Realtor's office." He glanced at his watch. "Say twenty minutes." Davis didn't wait for his brother's reply. He yanked the door open and left the cafe.

Angie placed a white mug of coffee in front of Josh and he thanked her. "What do you suggest to go with it?"

"We have cake, muffins, pies, sweet rolls. What do you like, anything in particular?"

Josh's face lit up and he chuckled. "I like everything."

Angie thought. "Well, how about a piece of pear frangipane tart?"

"Pear what?" Josh grinned.

"I'll give you a tiny slice to try," Angie told him. "If you don't like it, then I'll get you something else." She went to the bakery case and took a small plate down from the shelf.

A cell phone buzzed from Lisa's purse. The women always kept their bags under the front counter for safe keeping. They didn't like their wallets in the back room when delivery people were coming and going.

Lisa was pouring water from a big container into

the coffeemaker. "Could you grab that, Angie? I'm expecting a call from my allergist." Lisa was allergic to everything, mold, dust, pollen, and with the spring plants in bloom, she was really suffering. Her sinuses were blocked and her eyes always looked watery and red.

Lisa's purse was open so Angie reached inside for the phone to pass it to her. As she pulled it out, the bag wobbled and tipped over, emptying some of the contents onto the floor.

"Ugh." Angie moaned and passed the cell phone to Lisa. Angie bent to pick up the things that had fallen from the purse. Courtney leaned down to help, as Lisa took the call. They replaced her change purse, tissue packet, allergy pill container, eye drops, and checkbook.

"I hope I'm not going to be clumsy all day." Angie rolled her eyes.

Courtney giggled. "Clumsy isn't the best trait to have when you're serving customers their hot drinks."

With the purse back under the counter, Angie reached into the bakery case and cut a small piece of the pear tart. She placed it on the plate and carried it over to Josh.

"Are you always a klutz?" His eyes were mischievous.

Angie put a hand on her hip. "Only, now and then. You'd better stand back when I refill your coffee."

Josh chuckled. He picked up his fork and took a bite of the dessert. He closed his eyes and moaned.

Angie smiled, admiring the chiseled features of Josh's face. "Does that mean you like it?"

Josh opened his eyes. "It means I love it. I'd love a bigger piece, please."

Angie was about to cut another slice for him when Lisa called out to her. Lisa was holding the café's phone in her hand. Her face was pinched with worry. "Angie. It's Police Chief Martin. He says for you to come quick. It's Professor Linden. She's hurt. At her house. She's asking for you."

Angie's eyes went wide. Her heart jumped into her throat. She dropped the knife she was holding onto the counter and bolted from the bake shop.

2

Angie was still wearing her pink apron when she raced past four store fronts on Main Street and turned left onto Beach Street. Running past several small shops and residential houses, Angie could see a police car and an ambulance in front of Professor Linden's Victorian home. A crowd of people had gathered on the sidewalk opposite the house.

"Angie!" Police Chief Martin raised his hand to flag her over. An emergency medical technician was kneeling next to the professor who was on her side laying on the walkway next to the front stairs of her house.

"What's happened?" Angie was nearly breathless when she ran up the chief.

Two EMTs rolled a stretcher out of the ambulance and hurried it towards Professor Linden.

"A passerby saw the professor on the ground and called 911. The person said the professor seemed to be convulsing or having a seizure." The chief took Angie's elbow and quickly guided her over to the elderly woman prone on the ground. "The professor called for you," he told her.

Angie rushed to the older woman and knelt beside her. She swallowed hard to clear the worry from her voice. "Professor? It's me. It's Angie." She reached for Professor Linden's hand.

The professor's eyes fluttered open. "Angie." Her voice was barely more than a whisper. She squeezed Angie's hand. "Take care of my cat."

Angie blinked. "Yes. Yes, of course, I will. You'll be good as new soon. I'll take care of him until you're home again."

The tension of Professor Linden's fingers on Angie's hand eased and the muscles fell slack. The professor's eyes closed and she took a quick breath, almost a small hiccup, and then she was still. Angie looked at the tiny hand she was holding. Her gaze flicked to Professor Linden's face and then back to the hand. A sob caught in Angie's throat. Tears welled in her eyes and spilled over the lids, running down her cheeks.

Chief Martin placed a hand on Angie's shoulder and gave her a small squeeze.

On that bright, warm April morning, the professor was gone.

THE COUNTY CORONER was called and a car was sent over to retrieve the professor's body. Angie sat on the front steps of the Victorian as the attendants brought a stretcher from the coroner's vehicle and placed the body on it. A long strand of Angie's hair had come loose from her topknot and framed one side of her tear-stained face. The EMTs had covered Professor Linden's body with a sheet. One of the town's police officers was directing people to move along to keep them from stopping and gawking at the sad scene.

When the attendants rolled the stretcher across the lawn and moved it into the car, Angie stood and watched the vehicle drive away. She dabbed at her eyes as the chief approached. He had a set of keys in his hand.

"The cat. The professor's cat is in the house."
Chief Martin's shoulders drooped and the muscles
of his face sagged.

Angie stared at him, his words not registering
with her.

"Professor Linden asked you to take care of him."
The chief held up the keys. "The cat."

"Oh, right." Angie shook herself. "Yes." She
looked at the house. "Poor Euclid."

"Who?" the chief asked.

"Euclid. Her cat. That's his name."

They walked up the front stairs to the porch.

"How old was Professor Linden?" Angie asked.

"I really don't know. I've known her for years, but
never knew her age." The chief had grown up in
Sweet Cove and knew just about everybody from
town. He'd even known Angie when she was a little
girl and came to town with her sisters to visit their
grandmother. The chief put the key in the lock and
turned. It clicked and he pushed the door open.

Angie asked, "Did the professor have epilepsy? Is
that why she had a seizure?"

The chief shrugged. "I don't know that either."

"I know that her husband and son passed away
before her. And a brother too," Angie said. "Is there

someone who should be called? A relative? A friend?"

As they entered the foyer, the chief shook his head. "I don't know anything. I only know that Blake Ford was her attorney. He handled her affairs. I'll call him and let him know what happened. He'll know who to contact."

"But ...." Angie said.

"Oh, right," the chief said. "I keep forgetting that Blake's retired now and gone to Florida. His nephew has taken over the firm."

Angie wasn't sure calling the law office a "firm" was correct since it was only a one-lawyer operation.

The chief hooked his thumb into his belt. "I'll call the nephew. His last name's Ford. It's Jack Ford." He gestured for Angie to enter the house. "You meet him yet?"

Angie shook her head. "No. I don't think I've seen him around."

"He seems odd."

They glanced around for the cat.

Even though Angie had been in the Professor's home several times, the house never failed to impress her. The foyer of the Victorian had gleaming hardwood floors and high ceilings. A chandelier hung in the center of the space. There was a carved rectangular wooden table standing in the middle of the foyer with a large cut glass vase filled with tall colorful flowers. Carpets of cream, cranberry, and green were placed here and there over the floor. A large staircase led from the foyer to the second floor landing. The Victorian was perfectly decorated with period furniture, wallpapers, lamps, antiques, and mirrors. Entering the mansion was like stepping back into another era.

A terrible shriek came from the dining room on the right side of the foyer. Angie and the chief both jumped. The professor's orange cat was on top of the large China cabinet and he was staring at the two intruders who had dared to enter his home.

"Oh, it's only Euclid." Angie let out a breath. "It's me, little one. You scared me to death," she told the cat. The cat did not fit the category of "little one." He was a huge long-haired orange and white giant. The professor said he was part Maine Coon cat.

As the chief approached the tall cabinet, the cat arched its back. The chief took a step back, and then turned to Angie. "Ah, how shall we get him down?"

"Should I take him home or just come by each day to take care of him?" Angie looked up at Euclid.

"What do you think is best?" The chief eyed the cat.

"Maybe I'll come by here for a few days to start with," Angie said. "If Euclid seems amenable to me, then I'll take him to my apartment. You think that's okay? I can stop by the police station to pick up the key each morning and return it at the end of the day."

"Works for me." The chief handed Angie the keys. "Drop them off at the station when you're done here this evening." He moved towards the front door. "Thanks, Angie."

A thought popped into Angie's head. "Chief?"

The chief paused and turned to her.

"Why was the coroner called? Why not the funeral home?"

"It's the law," the chief said.

Angie's brow furrowed in confusion.

"The coroner must be called...when there are questions surrounding the death."

Angie took a step forward. "What do you mean 'questions'? Didn't the professor just die of natural causes?"

The chief looked down. "Right now, it falls into the category of 'unexplained.'"

"Why?" Angie's hand trembled causing the keys she was holding to jiggle.

"I can't say more, Angie. The coroner needs to look into it."

Angie's eyes were questioning. "Is it suspicious?" Her voice shook a little. "Do you think she didn't die of natural causes?"

The chief moved his hand in the air. He forced a slight smile. "It's just because it happened suddenly. That's all. Thanks for your help with the cat." He nodded, opened the door and stepped out onto the porch.

Angie stood in the foyer thinking over what the chief had said. A flutter of anxiety picked at her.

Euclid let out a meow.

Angie looked up at the cat and sighed. "It's just you and me, Euclid. For a while, anyway." Angie walked down the main hallway to the kitchen. She cleaned the cat box, freshened the water in the cat's bowl, and filled his dish with kibble. Euclid padded into the room and watched Angie complete the tasks.

"I have to go back to work now. I'll check on you later." Euclid followed Angie to the front door. Before leaving, she bent to scratch the cat's cheek and he started to purr.

"I'm sorry about the professor, Euclid. She was a nice lady."

Angie left the Victorian and headed back to the bake shop. She would miss Professor Linden's morning visits. Sadness gave Angie's heart a squeeze and tears gathered in her eyes.

3

Angie returned to the bake shop and when she opened the door, everyone turned to her and the questions started.

"Is it true about the professor?"

"Has she passed away?"

"Was it foul play?"

"The coroner was called?"

"What happened to her?"

Angie wished she could have just gone home to her apartment instead of having to come back to the shop. The barrage of questions unsettled her and intensified the feelings of sadness and shock that she was feeling. She stood in the doorway, her eyes wide. Worry lines creased her forehead.

Courtney was standing behind the serving

counter with a coffee pot in her hand. Lisa's arms were crossed over her chest with her hands clutching her forearms. Both of the women's faces were pinched with concern. Lisa looked like she was trembling.

Angie told Courtney, Lisa, and the customers what had happened, which set off another round of questions and discussion. Angie said that she didn't have any more information and the cause of death was unknown which is why the coroner was involved.

Courtney could see the strain on Angie's face and she hurried to her side. She slipped her arm around Angie's waist and ushered her to a table in the corner.

"Thanks for the rescue," Angie murmured to her sister.

"Sit down for a while. I'll get you some tea." Courtney hurried to the counter to prepare a hot beverage.

The customers realized that their peppering of questions had flustered Angie and had increased her distress. They turned to each other to continue their speculations about the professor's unexpected passing.

Courtney returned to the table with a cup of tea

for Angie and sat down in the seat opposite her older sister. "Do the police suspect foul play?" Courtney kept her voice low.

"I don't know." Angie's fingers shook as she reached for the cup and lifted it to her lips. She sipped the tea. "It wasn't so much what the chief said to me that worried me. It was more the expression on his face and what he didn't say. He seemed very concerned. It made me think something was wrong." Angie rubbed her temples. "We'll just have to see what comes out. Hopefully, the professor died from nothing more than natural causes, which is upsetting enough."

"I can't believe she's gone." Courtney looked out the window. "I can't believe she won't be coming through that door tomorrow morning." Her eyes misted over.

Angie reached for Courtney's hand.

THE REST of the day passed quietly as the women tended customers, cleaned the shop, and made preparations for the following morning's opening. At three o'clock, they locked up the cafe and Angie and Courtney walked along Main Street towards Angie's apartment. Angie's shoulders and neck muscles were tight and sore and her whole body felt sluggish and fatigued.

Courtney wanted to make her sister feel better. "Listen, why don't we go for a bike ride? The day is still warm. The exercise would do us good. It might help lift our spirits."

Angie put her arm over Courtney's shoulders. "I haven't biked for months. It's a great idea. Let's do it. That is, if you're not afraid of pulling the bikes out of the creepy basement."

"Hmm. Why don't you get the bikes out of storage, and I'll pack snacks and water for us." Courtney smiled.

Angie grinned. "I'm not surprised by that suggestion knowing how fond you are of cobwebs and bugs."

When they reached Angie's apartment house, they climbed the stairs to the second floor one bedroom place. It was a small, but cozy space with a living room, bedroom with two single beds, small bathroom, and a galley kitchen. It had three big windows in the living room which allowed maximum natural light to flood the room. There was a non-working fireplace on one wall and Angie had hung a large photograph of herself and her three sisters above the mantel.

The picture showed the four girls at the Sweet Cove beach and there was no denying that they were siblings, each one with bright blue eyes and hair in varying shades from pale blonde to light brown. On the day the photograph was taken, they had just finished playing a game of Frisbee when their mother snapped the picture catching their high energy and cheerful spirits.

Jenna was Angie's fraternal twin, born three minutes after Angie, and even though a resemblance was strong, no one ever believed that they were twins. Angie's honey blonde hair had a slight wave to it and Jenna's light brown hair was as straight as a stick. Angie stood five feet six inches but Jenna was three inches taller.

Ellie was three years younger than the twins and was nearly as tall as Jenna. Her height and light blonde hair gave her a Scandinavian appearance. Courtney was the youngest, born three years after Ellie. Her height and hair color was closer to Angie's, but Courtney's hair was as straight as Jenna's.

The girls and their mother had spent many happy summers at Sweet Cove staying at their grandmother's small cottage out on Robin's Point. It was a tight squeeze fitting all of them into the tiny house, but Angie couldn't remember happier times than when they were all together there. When Angie was twelve, her grandmother passed away and the cottage was sold. After that, the girls and their mother only came to Sweet Cove for day trips or an occasional weekend.

Angie dropped her canvas bag on the floor next to the sofa and kicked off her shoes.

"Let's change fast." Courtney tossed her sweater on the chair. "Then we can get in at least an hour of biking before dusk."

Angie's heart ached with the sadness of Professor Linden's passing and she just wanted to crawl into bed and take a nap, but she took a deep breath and went to the bedroom to put on her exercise clothes.

THE SKY WAS STREAKED with pinks and violet when the girls returned from their ride as the sun was sinking behind the treetops. Exercising outdoors was just what Angie needed and she felt much less stressed when returning the bikes to the storage area in the basement. She decided she would go to check on Euclid after showering and eating some dinner.

Angie chopped tomatoes, onions, and peppers
and heated them in a frying pan while Courtney
made garlic bread and warmed up tomato soup.
Angie cracked eggs into a bowl with a bit of salt and
beat them with a whisk for a few seconds. She
poured them into the pan and swirled them with the
veggies. When the omelets had firmed up, Angie
sprinkled them with cheese and removed the pan
from the burner. The girls took their plates of food
and bowls of soup and curled up on the sofa to eat
their dinner and talk.

"I need to go take care of Euclid," Angie said
after devouring the food.

"Do you want me to come?" Courtney wiped
some soup from her chin.

"No, I'll go over myself. You concentrate on your
schoolwork. I know you have that paper to write."
Angie stood and started to gather up the dishes but
Courtney waved her off.

"Go on. Go see the cat. I'll handle clean-up. I'll go
with you in the morning to see him on our way to
the bake shop." Angie gave her sister a hug, grabbed
a sweater, and headed off to see Euclid.

Approaching Beach Street, a sinking feeling of
sadness pulled at Angie's stomach and she slowed
her pace. The image of the professor lying on the

brick walkway at the foot of her home's front steps flashed in Angie's mind. She tried to shake the mental picture from her brain. Streetlights illuminated the darkening sidewalks and the warmth of the day had dissipated leaving a chill in the evening air.

The Victorian was shrouded in darkness. Climbing the front stairs to the wraparound porch, Angie pulled the key from her pocket. Low-level anxiety pricked at her as she inserted the key into the lock and she hoped there wasn't a security alarm system that no one told her about. That's all she would need, a screeching alarm going off while Euclid careened through the house as Angie desperately looked for how to turn it off.

Opening the door, she braced herself and then let out a sigh of relief when the house remained silent. Her hand fumbled along the wall trying to find the light switch, and touching it, she flicked it on and lit up the foyer. The beauty of the space calmed her and her muscles relaxed. She hadn't realized how wound up she was until the tension in her body eased a little.

"Euclid?" Angie glanced into the dining room for the cat. She turned to the left of the entrance and headed for the living room. She turned on one of the lamps that stood on a side table and the light cast a warm glow over the room.

"Here, kitty. Euclid?" The room was empty of any feline presence. *I hope I don't have to search eighteen rooms looking for him.*

Angie decided to head for the kitchen. She walked through the foyer, and turned down the hall that led to the back of the house. She couldn't find a light switch so she placed her palm on the wall and felt her way along into the kitchen. The room was black except for a tiny bit of starlight coming through the window. *Where's the darn switch?* She decided that she would bring a flashlight next time she came to the house at night.

A crash from the second floor rocked the quiet and Angie jumped. Her heart started to race and a flash of anxiety shot down her spine, but then she realized what must have caused the noise. The cat must have knocked something over upstairs. There was a second staircase in the kitchen and Angie thought there must be a light switch at the bottom of the steps so she edged through the dark kitchen to find it. Passing the kitchen table, two green glowing eyes stared at her. Angie yelped in surprise. She put her hand to her face and chuckled.

"Euclid. You need to stop scaring me." She shook

her head at how jumpy she was. She started to reach out to scratch Euclid's cheek when the thump of hurried footsteps from the front staircase caused Angie to freeze in place. Someone is in the house! Euclid turned towards the noise, arched his back, and hissed low in his throat. Panic flooded Angie's veins, fear practically choked her. She held her breath and listened trying to hear which way the footsteps were headed. The foyer wood floor creaked. The front door opened and shut. A rush of air escaped from Angie's lungs. Who had been in the house?

The back door opened behind her with a creak. A scream escaped from Angie's throat.

4

A figure stepped into the kitchen through the back door. The person let out a piercing scream in concert with Angie's shriek. The open door let a stream of moonlight into the dark kitchen and recognition stopped Angie's panic.

Gasping, she said, "Courtney. I didn't know it was you. I didn't know who was coming through the door."

"You scared the heck out of me," Courtney said, her breathing quick and shallow. She had her hand pressed against her chest over her heart. "Why are you standing in the dark screaming?"

"I couldn't find the light." Angie wheezed.

Courtney felt along the wall, found the switch plate and turned on the lights.

Angie let out a long breath and plopped onto one of the kitchen chairs, rubbing her forehead.

"What's wrong with you? You're screaming because you can't find the light switch?" Courtney stood in front of her sister trying to understand what was going on.

Angie stood up abruptly. "Someone was in the house. Upstairs. I was in here and I heard a crash, then someone's footsteps on the front staircase. Whoever it was, he left through the front door. I was terrified. Then you came in through the back and scared me to death."

Courtney stepped closer to her sister, her eyes wide. "Who was it? Who could it have been? He must have heard you in here and took off." She took hold of Angie's arm. "Come on." She tugged Angie towards the hallway. "Let's go upstairs and see what he was doing up there."

Angie hesitated. "I don't know. We need to go and lock the front door. Oh, wait. Lock the back door first."

Courtney's blue eyes were blazing with anger over the intruder. She asked Angie, "Where's your phone? Call the police. Report it. No one is supposed to be in this house."

Angie reached for her phone and made the call to the police while her sister locked the back door.

"Where's Euclid?" Angie looked around the kitchen. "He was right here. He heard the person, too. He was hissing."

"Let's see if he's in the dining room." Courtney led the way through the hall and back into the foyer. They locked the front door and then searched the two front rooms without locating the cat. A meow from upstairs brought the young women to the bottom of the staircase. Euclid was looking down at them from the second floor landing.

"Come on. Let's go see." Angie and Courtney climbed to the second floor.

When they reached the top, Angie pointed and said, "Look over there." A door was open to one of the rooms off the landing that the professor had obviously used as an office. A roll top desk's drawers were open. Several mahogany file cabinets lined one wall and the drawers were pulled open, the contents hanging in disheveled disarray. Some manila folders and papers were strewn across the floor.

Euclid was standing in the doorway peering into the room.

"Who would do this? What were they looking for?" Angie's brow furrowed as her eyes swept over the room.

The doorbell chimed.

"The police." Courtney started down the stairs. "I'll let them in and bring them up."

Chief Martin and Officer Talbot entered the mansion. Angie called out a greeting to them from the landing and they climbed the steps to the second floor. Angie explained what had happened and pointed to the study. The police stepped into the room. They took some photographs. Angie and Courtney stood at the edge of the den watching the police investigate.

"Doesn't look like any damage, but it will be nearly impossible to tell if anything's missing since the only person who could tell us has passed away." The chief shook his head. "I'll get a locksmith out here in the morning. It can't hurt to change the locks. Get something more secure on the doors. And, the windows."

"Did you speak to the lawyer? Are there any relatives?" Angie asked.

"I left him a message. I haven't heard back. I'll pay him a visit tomorrow morning." The police officers finished up taking the photos and then they all returned to the foyer. "We'll head outside now to look around." The chief flicked on a heavy, black flashlight.

"I haven't fed the cat yet," Angie said. "Should I drop the key at the station once I finish up here?"

"I'd like to stick around until you're done with the cat and then drive you two home," the chief said. "Officer Talbot and I are going to check the back of the house, look around the grounds. Let me know when you're ready to head out."

Officer Talbot was inspecting the front door while the chief spoke to the girls. "Chief, there's no sign of forced entry here."

"Oh, wait." Angie thought of something. "The back door was unlocked. That's how the intruder must have gotten in."

Courtney nodded. "I came in that way, too. I thought Angie left the door unlocked."

Angie shook her head. "I came in through the front. The back door must have been unlocked all day. I didn't think to check it before I left to go back to work this morning. That must be how the intruder got inside."

The chief's eyes narrowed and his forehead creased. "No. I made sure the back door was closed and locked when I left you here earlier today. The suspect must have forced the lock and come in that way. We'll have a look. We'll send a couple of officers over tomorrow to straighten up the upstairs room."

The officers went outside to make a check of the property while Angie and Courtney tended the cat. When they were getting ready to lock up and head home, Angie gave Euclid a pointed look.

"I wish you could talk, Euclid. I'm sure you'd have a lot to tell us."

Euclid trilled at them.

"Goodnight, kitty," Courtney said. She petted the top of the orange cat's head.

The girls met the chief outside. He told them, "There isn't any evidence that someone forced the back door. Either the intruder has a key or he knows how to pick a lock. That's how the door was open."

Angie's face clouded with worry.

"We'll get the locksmith here first thing in the morning. We'll get something sturdy on the doors and windows." As they headed for the police car, the chief added, "Wouldn't hurt to look into getting a security system installed. I'll speak to Attorney Ford about getting that done."

Angie thought that a security system was a good idea. Who knew how long the Victorian would be empty.

The chief drove the young women the few blocks to their apartment in the patrol car and saw them safely inside.

COURTNEY AND ANGIE put on their pajamas, made tea, and curled up on the sofa. Courtney pulled a blanket over her legs. "I need to work on my paper for my class. I'll do it right after I finish my tea."

"How did you decide to come to the professor's house tonight?" Angie asked.

"I loaded the dinner dishes in the dishwasher and just didn't feel like doing schoolwork. I decided to walk over to the house and see the cat."

"I'm glad you did. I was never so happy to see you." Angie hugged her arms around herself remembering the terror of hearing someone in the house.

"What do you think about it?" Courtney sipped from her mug.

"I don't know." Angie pulled part of the blanket over her knees. "I wonder if it was someone who heard that Professor Linden had died and got the idea to break in looking for money or valuables. The person probably knew that the professor lived alone, didn't have relatives in the area. He must have assumed that the house would be empty, so it was a perfect time to break in and rob the place."

"It makes sense." Courtney frowned. "It's sad. It must be someone from Sweet Cove. No one else would have known yet. There hasn't been time for a death notice in the papers."

The thought that someone from the little town would do such a thing gave Angie a chill. "You're right. Word about her death spread through town today. Someone decided to break in before a friend or relative could be notified and take possession of the house. It's just awful to think that someone from town would do something like that."

"There are creeps everywhere," Courtney said. She placed her mug on the little coffee table in front of the sofa.

"I wonder what they stole. What they took." Angie's brow furrowed. "I guess we'll never know."

5

The café was in full swing with customers coming and going, conversations at full volume, and Angie, Courtney, and Lisa alternating between making drinks, serving treats, cleaning off tables, and ringing up sales.

The door opened and a young man who looked to be in his early thirties entered the café. He stood straight, his eyes darting over the patrons for several seconds. The man was slim, had close-cut brown hair, big eyes, and a pale face. He wore black rimmed glasses and had on a brown tweed jacket. There was a red bow tie at his neck.

Angie was behind the counter serving a choco-late croissant to Tom, one of her regular customers. Tom owned a building and carpentry business in town and he came in every morning for coffee before heading off to his projects. He was a little older than Angie, with strong shoulders and large hands. The two of them enjoyed chatting and cheerfully teasing each other. Tom spotted the man and leaned forward to speak to Angie in a quiet voice.

"That's the new lawyer. Jack Ford's his name. He's the nephew of Blake Ford. I went to see Ford recently to have him handle some legal work for me. I didn't like him. He's odd, seems sort of stuck up. Thinks he's a smarty pants. He's not like his uncle, not by a long shot."

Angie glanced at the newcomer and wondered why he was just standing near the door. She re-filled Tom's coffee and was turning away, when the lawyer approached the counter. His movements were clipped and quick like he was trying to conserve energy by not making any extraneous motions. Angie looked up, the coffee pot still in her hand, just as the attorney spoke.

"Angela Roseland?" His voice was firm and formal.

Angie nodded. Courtney sidled up next to her sister wondering what this man wanted. Tom swiveled on his stool and eyed the guy.

"This is a letter for you requesting your presence

at the reading of Professor Marion Linden's will. Tomorrow at eleven in the morning." He held the envelope out to her.

Angie blinked and stared at him. She didn't reach for the letter. "You're the ...?"

Before she could finish her question, the man said, "I'm Jack Ford. Professor Linden's legal representative."

Angie looked at the envelope that he held out, but didn't take it. "Why would I be asked to the reading of the will?"

"Because, Ms. Roseland." The attorney placed the envelope on the counter. He adjusted the lapel of his jacket. "You are mentioned in the will."

Conversations became quiet and many patrons turned their heads to look at Angie and the lawyer who were standing on opposite sides of the counter.

As the lawyer turned to leave, he gave a slight nod of his head. "We will see you tomorrow."

Angie watched the attorney exit the café. She shifted her gaze to the envelope. Customers started talking again in hushed tones.

"See," Tom said, shaking his head. "He's a weird-o."

Courtney picked up the envelope and turned it over in her hand. She held it out to Angie who took it and stared at it. "Why would I be mentioned in the will?"

Tom took a swig of his coffee and said, "Maybe she left you her fortune." He chuckled and Angie gave him a nervous smile.

"Open it," Courtney said. "Let's see what it says."

Angie opened the envelope and read the enclosed letter. She handed it to Courtney. "It's just an invitation. Just like, he said."

Courtney read, "The last will and testament of Marion Linden will be read at Professor Linden's home at 32 Beach Street, Sweet Cove, Massachusetts, tomorrow at eleven o'clock in the morning." She raised her eyes to Angie. "You're going, aren't you?"

Angie nodded. "Can you go back to school a day later? I'd like you to come with me."

"You don't need to ask me twice. You bet I'll go with you." Courtney moved to the register to ring up a sale.

Tom grinned at Angie and teased. "Want me to come, too?"

Angie gave him a mock scowl and said, "I'm only allowed one guest."

"Darn. I was hoping to share in your riches." Tom winked at her and went back to reading his newspaper.

"I'm NERVOUS." Angie reached into her black blazer for her phone which she silenced. She wore black slacks and a crisp white blouse under her jacket. Her honey blonde hair fell in soft waves around her shoulders.

"You don't need to be nervous." Courtney had borrowed her sister's black skirt and tights and wore a pale blue sweater. She had her long caramel hair pulled into a high ponytail which swished from side to side as she walked.

"I know it isn't logical, but I'm still nervous." Angie smoothed her hair with a shaky hand. "It's just because I don't know what to expect."

"Professor Linden liked you. You were nice to her. She probably has a favorite piece of jewelry that she wants you to have."

Angie's eyes got misty. "That would be so thoughtful of her."

The sisters turned onto the brick walkway that led to the steps and wraparound porch of the Victorian mansion. The front door was open so they entered into the foyer. There were two rows of chairs set up in the living room and a number of people had already arrived. Some had taken seats and several people were conversing standing by the windows. Angie recognized most of the people in the room from town and from being her customers, and she greeted them with a smile and joined one of the groups.

"Ladies and gentlemen." Jack Ford entered the room dressed in a similar outfit to what he wore when he delivered the envelope to Angie at her bake shop, only today his bow tie was yellow with blue polka dots. "Please take your seats and we will begin."

People shuffled to sit down and once everyone was settled, Jack Ford cleared his throat and stood in front of the small gathering. "I will read aloud Professor Linden's wishes." He began to read from a document that he was holding.

"Thank you, all of you, for coming today. As most of you know, my dear husband, beloved son, and brother predeceased me and I have no family left. The town of Sweet Cove has been a special place for me and I consider many of you old friends and others of you, new friends. I have appreciated your kindness as I have grown older therefore, I wish to thank you by leaving town departments part of my estate. To the Sweet Cove Public Library, I leave fifty thousand dollars." The head librarian gasped and lifted her hand to her mouth. Jack Ford shot her a disapproving look. He went on, "To the Sweet Cove Police Department and Emergency Services, I leave one hundred thousand dollars." Chief Martin's eyes went wide. The attorney went on listing several other bequests to town departments and charities, the museum, the school, and the historical society.

Courtney leaned close to Angie. "Who knew the professor was so wealthy?"

"To my alma mater and the university where I worked for over thirty years, I leave one million dollars." A buzz of surprise filled the room. Several times, Attorney Ford had to ask for quiet. He continued. "And, finally." He looked over his glasses at Angie for a half second. "I leave my beloved Victorian home, property, and all of its contents to Angela Roseland."

Angie's eyes went wide and she gasped. Courtney's jaw dropped.

"As well as seventy-five thousand dollars to Ms. Roseland to make the necessary changes to the house to suit her needs. In addition, I leave my dear cat, Euclid, to Ms. Roseland. I trust she will treat him with kindness and love."

The edges of Angie's vision were sparkling and her head was spinning. She blinked hard several

times, and then she swayed and keeled over out of
her seat. She hit the floor with a soft thud. The last
thing Angie heard was Attorney Ford saying, "And
this concludes the reading of Professor Marion
Linden's will."

Angie opened her eyes to see a crowd of people
peering down at her. Courtney slipped her hand
under her sister's arm and helped Angie to sitting
position. "Good thing you wore slacks today since
you ended up on the floor," she gently kidded her
sister.

Someone brought a glass of water and handed it
to Courtney to pass to Angie. Angie put her trembling hand to her head. A blush of embarrassment
tinged her cheeks pink.

"Here. Have a sip of water and then we'll help
you into a chair." Courtney handed Angie the glass.

"I'm so sorry. I was just so...." Angie took a sip
from the glass.

"It's okay," Chief Martin said. He helped Angie
stand and maneuvered her back onto her chair. "It's
all very surprising."

Attorney Ford made an announcement. "Probate
information will be filed with the courts immedi-
ately and I expect everything will be settled in about
sixty to ninety days. At that time, checks will be

going out to all of you. Thank you for coming. Miss Roseland, a word please?"

Attorney Ford stepped to the side of the room. Angie stood shakily and walked over to join him. Ford said, "Professor Linden indicated in her will that she would like you to have immediate access to the house, moving in right away if you so wished. During the probate period, you may live here in the house free of charge. I will designate you as caretaker. That is, if these arrangements are acceptable to you."

Angie nodded. Her vision was still blurry.

Attorney Ford continued, "Of course, any changes you choose to make to the dwelling will have to wait until the deed to the house is in your possession." He handed Angie the keys to the house. "Enjoy your new home. The deed to the house will be enclosed with the check that you receive in a couple of months." Ford paused for a moment as if there might be more he wanted to say. A jolt of unease washed over Angie as something passed between them. Attorney Ford gave an almost imperceptible nod of his head, wheeled towards the door, and left.

The remaining people in attendance chatted for a few minutes and then slowly made their way out of the Victorian leaving Angie and Courtney alone in the house. They sat side by side next to the window in matching antique chairs.

A wide grin spread over Courtney's face. "This is all yours. It's your house, Angie. No mortgage. It belongs to you, free and clear. You'll be the official owner in two or three months." She let out a whoop.

Angie rubbed her forehead. "I'm in a state of shock. Is this a dream? Why would she leave the house to me?"

"She knew how you always admired the house. She knew you were losing the shop and that you wanted to stay in Sweet Cove." Courtney put her hand on her sister's arm. "You were always kind to her."

Angie shook her head in disbelief. Out of nowhere, Euclid jumped onto Angie's lap and trilled. Angie chuckled and patted the huge, orange cat. "Where did you come from, Euclid?" He settled in Angie's lap, purring. "Looks like you're stuck with me, buddy."

"I think Euclid is pleased," Courtney told her sister. They sat for a few moments listening to the cat's loud, calming purrs.

Courtney sat up. "Angie, you can move the café here. The house is only a block away from where the café is now. You'd get all the foot traffic from people going to the beach. And all your regulars only have to walk around the corner. It's perfect."

Angie's eyes sparkled. "That's a fantastic idea. Professor Linden left me the money. I could do renovations to outfit a café." Angie thought of their other two sisters and shifted a little in her seat being careful not to disturb Euclid who was snoozing in her lap. She faced Courtney. "Jenna and Ellie. We could all move in here together. There's more than enough room and there's the carriage house out back too."

Courtney's eyes went wide with excitement. "All of us together again. Jenna could move her jewelry shop here. She'd only need one room on the first floor for a shop. Oh, and Ellie has always wanted to run a bed and breakfast. You could set aside some rooms for guests. There's so much space. You could do all that and still have plenty of rooms left over for private quarters for all of us. You know how Jenna and Ellie both love Sweet Cove. They'd love to live here."

"It's perfect," Angie whispered as gratitude rose in her chest and tears welled in her eyes. "The wrap around porch would be a wonderful place to put some café seating out there. People love to sit outdoors and have coffee. I can't believe this." Some tears spilled down her cheeks. "Someone needs to pinch me."

"Meow," Euclid said, and then he went back to purring in Angie's lap.

"Euclid thinks it's a great idea, too." The two young women laughed. Courtney scratched the cat's cheek and his purring grew louder.

Angie ran her hand over Euclid's soft, orange coat. "We need to call Jenna and Ellie. We need to tell them the good news."

6

When they got the call from Angie, Jenna and Ellie each packed a bag, jumped in Jenna's car and headed for Sweet Cove. Jenna was an independent jewelry maker who worked out of her apartment and sold her designs online. She filled a suitcase with her beads and tools so that she could continue to work while she was with her sisters. Ellie had graduated from college three years ago with a degree in business and was working in a Boston hotel in a junior management position. She notified her supervisor that she would be away for a few days in regards to a family emergency. She stretched the truth a bit with that, but she considered that all emergencies didn't have to fall into a negative category.

When they pulled into the Victorian's driveway, Angie and Courtney were sitting on the front porch in rocking chairs waiting for their sisters to arrive. They jumped up out of the rockers and hurried down the porch steps to welcome the girls.

"I can't believe that you own the Victorian." Jenna hugged Angie. "It's a dream come true."

"Well, it's not official. I don't own it yet, but in about two or three months I will," Angie said.

Jenna waved her hand in the air. "It's as good as done."

Ellie hugged Courtney and they pulled suitcases from the trunk. Staring up at the beautiful Victorian house, Ellie had a wide grin on her face. "How is this possible? I feel like I'm in a dream."

The four sisters went into the mansion and greeted Euclid. Angie gave the girls a tour with the cat following behind them. Wandering from room to room, Ellie and Jenna ooh-ed and aah-ed over the space, the furnishings, and the paintings on the walls.

"I'm still learning my way around the house," Angie said. "The amount of space is ridiculous. And there are more furniture pieces, artwork, and boxes in the attic that will take the rest of our lives to go through." She showed them where she wanted to open her café and where she thought Jenna would like to set up her jewelry shop.

She told Ellie all about her ideas for the bed and breakfast spaces which would use the first floor living room, dining room, kitchen and bath and five bedrooms and baths on the second floor. Angie said, "The third floor could serve as our private space. It has a central room that we could use as our living room and then there are two baths and six other rooms. We can split it up any way we want and there's the carriage house out back, too. That's set up as two separate apartments each with two bedrooms."

Jenna plopped into a chair. "I'm stunned."

Tears ran down Ellie's cheeks and Courtney gripped her arm. "Are you okay?"

Ellie nodded but couldn't speak for a moment, her throat clogged with emotion. She swallowed and wiped the tears from her face. "I just can't believe it. I always dreamed of running a bed and breakfast. I never in a million years believed that it would come true." She pushed a strand of her blonde hair away from her eyes. "Thank you, Angie."

Angie, Courtney, and Jenna were all near tears themselves. "This calls for a group hug," Angie said.

They huddled together, their arms around each other.

THE GIRLS WERE in the kitchen preparing dinner when the doorbell sounded.

"I'll go see." Angie wiped her hands on a dish towel and headed to the front door, Euclid tagging along behind her. The person on the doorstep caused Angie to stiffen, wondering what he wanted.

"Hello," said Davis Williams. He was wearing black slacks, a pale blue shirt, and a dark gray jacket. Angie saw his silver Mercedes parked at the end of the driveway. "Sorry to interrupt. Do you have a minute to speak?"

Angie wondered if he wanted her to vacate the bake shop earlier than what was planned. She had to stifle her annoyance. "Would you like to sit down?"

"Thank you."

They moved to the living room and Williams took a seat on one of the sofas and Angie sat in a straight-back chair opposite him. She waited for him to speak.

Williams made eye contact with Angie, and even

though he gave her a slight smile, she thought it looked insincere. "So, is everything going as scheduled for your move out of the premises?"

"Yes. Everything is planned and in place for me to move the bake shop out of your building in a few weeks." She was wondering where Williams was going with his question.

"Have you secured a new location?" Williams tapped his fingers on the arm of sofa.

"It's still up in the air." Angie didn't want to give him any information about her plans.

"Well, I hope you are able to stay in Sweet Cove. The coffee shop gives a nice bit of local flavor to the area."

Angie had no response to that. At least, nothing that was polite. If her shop gave the area important local flavor then why was Williams kicking her out of the building?

"As you know, my brother and I are developers and are always interested in the acquisition of important properties." Williams had his hands clasped in his lap and his index fingers were pointing upward and were tapping together lightly.

Angie waited.

"It's my understanding that you would like to find another place in Sweet Cove to locate your coffee shop but the spots that are available are quite expensive."

"It's not just a coffee shop," Angie corrected him. "It's also a bake shop and a cafe. We serve home-made soups and sandwiches, too."

"Yes. I see. So." Williams paused. Angie's comment seemed to throw him off topic for a moment. He cleared his throat. "Money, perhaps, is preventing you from choosing a new location?"

What on earth is he droning on about?

When Angie didn't reply, Williams said, "I understand that you have acquired the Linden Victorian."

Angie was amused that Williams spoke about the mansion like it was somewhere else in town, and wondered if he had forgotten that he was actually sitting in it. She had to tamp down a chuckle.

"Miss Roseland?"

Williams' voice pulled Angie back to the conversation. "Um, yes," she said. "Yes, I have, acquired it."

"Well. I'm prepared to make you a very generous offer for the building. I understand that the estate must be probated, but as soon as that's settled and you have the deed, we would like to proceed with the purchase." Williams gave Angie a thin smile.

"That is, should we come to agreeable terms, of course."

Angie's eyes widened. Oh, that's what this is about. She hadn't expected this, but she had to admit it made sense. She wasn't sure how to respond.

Euclid leaped up on the far end of the sofa. Williams jumped slightly at the cat's sudden appearance. "Oh. A cat." He couldn't hide the scowl that flickered over his face as he brushed an imaginary cat hair from the sleeve of his suit jacket.

Euclid glared at Williams.

Williams turned his attention back to Angie. "Yes. I'm prepared to make a very generous offer." He went on, keeping the cat in his peripheral vision. "An offer that will make you a very wealthy woman. In fact, it is an offer that would provide you with the opportunity to never have to work again. Should you invest smartly, of course." Williams nodded to punctuate his statements.

"I'm not planning on selling," Angie said.

Williams' face hardened. He was a man who was not often refused. "Perhaps, you'd like to hear the offer, Miss Roseland, before making a decision."

Angie shook her head. "No, thank you."

"Why don't I send over some paperwork for you to look over?" Williams persisted.

"That wouldn't change my mind." Angie stood up. "I want to be respectful of your time, and since I don't...."

Williams cut her off. "It certainly wouldn't hurt for you to entertain the offer. Understand that the dollar figure is only a starting point. We are prepared to negotiate, of course."

"But I have plans for the house," Angie said.

Williams snorted. "You realize the upkeep that a place like this requires? The taxes. The heating costs. The repairs. You would have to sell a great many lattes and cupcakes to be able to support a place like this."

Angie bristled.

Just then, Courtney walked into the room and stood next to her sister. Her arms were folded over her chest. Ellie entered next and stood beside Courtney. Jenna came in and took her place next to Ellie. None of the young women were smiling.

"These are my sisters, Mr. Williams. We're planning on living here together. We have a number of businesses that we plan to run out of the house. I think we'll be alright."

Williams leaned forward. His face muscles were

tense. "You understand that the offer isn't open-ended? The deal would have to be agreed upon quite quickly."

Angie nodded. "I understand, but we won't be considering any offers for the house. Thank you, anyway."

Williams was about to say something else, but Euclid stood up, arched his back, and gave a quick hiss. Williams got off the sofa in a hurry to get away from the cat.

"Thank you for coming," Angie said through gritted teeth. She walked Williams to the door.

Jenna leaned close to Euclid. "Good boy," she whispered and gave him a wink.

Angie closed the front door and locked it. She turned to her sisters and said, "I guess the big important real estate developer is afraid of a kitty cat." The four of them burst out laughing. Euclid flicked his tail, leaped off the sofa, and paraded away looking smug.

THE GIRLS finally sat down to a dinner of meat chili, veggie chili, salad, and garlic bread. It had been two months since the four of them were together and they chatted and chuckled for two hours.

They cleared the dishes, cleaned up and then returned to sit around the dining room table to make some plans. Each one had a pad of paper in front of them so that they could take notes on the tasks that had to be accomplished.

Courtney said. "I only have two things on my list. Number one is to graduate from college in a month and number two is to help all of you with your tasks."

Everyone laughed.

"We'll be glad to have your help," Jenna told her. "But if you don't get back to school, you won't accomplish number one on your list."

"You need to take the early train back to Boston tomorrow morning," Angie said. "You've missed two days of classes already."

Courtney groaned.

After an hour of list-making and discussion, the sisters were ready to wrap things up for the night and they decided to have tea and some of the almond cake that Angie made earlier in the day. Just as they had set out glass dishes, linen napkins and silver forks and spoons, the doorbell rang.

"Who could that be?" Jenna asked. "It's already past nine."

"It better not be that Davis Williams back again." Angie stood, crossed into the foyer and opened the front door. Chief Martin stood on the porch.

"May I come in, Angie?" His face looked somber.

Angie stepped back to let the chief into the foyer. "Of course, come in."

The chief saw the three young women clustered around the dining table. "Oh, I didn't know you had everyone here."

The girls stood up and he greeted Jenna and Ellie.

"Why don't you sit with us?" Angie suggested. "Have a slice of cake."

The chief shifted his feet and glanced down. "Oh, I don't know." He looked at Angie. "I need to speak with you. Privately."

A nervous chill ran across Angie's shoulders. The chief's face was pinched with worry and his demeanor told her that his news wasn't good. Angie would rather hear something bad with her sisters around her. She couldn't imagine what the chief had come to tell her. Was the will wrong? Is this house not going to belong to me? Her heart sank.

"Sit with us." Angie gestured to the table. "You

can speak in front of my sisters. I don't keep anything from them."

The chief gave a slight nod and took a seat at the table.

"Can I get you some tea? A cold drink?" Angie asked.

The chief shook his head. "No, thanks."

Angie sat down. The color had drained from her face. She braced herself for the bad news. News that she was sure would affect all of them.

"I got some news today." The chief cleared his throat. "It's about Professor Linden. The toxicology reports have come back." The girls sat on the edges of their seats. "The reports indicate that Professor Linden was poisoned."

Gasps escaped from the girls' throats.

Angie put her hand over her mouth. "How?" Her voice was barely above a whisper.

"Who did it?" Courtney said. "Do you have suspects?"

"Why would someone poison the professor?" Jenna asked.

The chief turned the palms of his meaty hands up. "I can't answer your questions. It's an ongoing investigation, so I can't say much. But...." He directed his attention to Angie.

"But, what?" Angie stiffened.

"Your name came up...on a list of people with possible motive."

Angie held on to the edges of the table with trembling fingers. "Me? Motive?"

"Why on earth would Angie be suspected?" Ellie's voice was indignant.

Realization dawned on all them.

"Oh," Jenna said. She reached over and squeezed Angie's hand. "Because you inherited the house."

Everyone sat in stunned silence for a few moments.

"But I didn't even know I was mentioned in the will." Angie sat up straighter. "How would I know that? I didn't have any idea that Professor Linden left the house to me."

"If Angie didn't know she would inherit the house from the professor then the motive disappears." Jenna looked at the chief for confirmation.

"Right," the chief said. "But it might be hard to convince someone that you didn't know."

"But I didn't." Angie's voice was almost shrill.

A terrible hissing noise came from the corner of the dining room and everyone turned to look. Euclid stood with the hairs on his back sticking up. He let out another hiss that was clearly directed at the chief. He leaped onto the sideboard and up to the top of the China cabinet, where he sat down. His green eyes glared at the chief.

Chief Martin adjusted himself in his chair and coughed. "I'll head out now. I wanted to let you know what was going on. There'll be questions, Angie. Investigators from the city will be here. They don't seem to think that a small force like Sweet Cove's is capable of handling a murder case." The girls winced at the word "murder."

The chief got up. "I'll keep you informed the best that I can," he told Angie. Jenna stood and walked the chief to the door.

"Thanks for coming," Angie managed from her seat. "Thanks for letting me know." Despite her words, her face didn't look thankful at all.

As soon as the door was closed, Angie crossed her arms on the table and laid her head on top of them.

"That's outrageous." Courtney stood up and started pacing around the room.

"How on earth can they put your name on a list of suspects?" Ellie asked. "You didn't know anything about the professor's will." Her blue eyes flashed.

Angie lifted her head. "It'll be okay. They'll just

ask me questions. It's probably a formality. They have no proof of anything."

"That's right," Jenna said. "Because, you didn't do anything. They'll probably talk to you and then move on to find the real killer. Everything will be okay."

"The professor," Angie said. "Murdered? It's unbelievable. Why would someone kill her? Poison her?" Angie shuddered at the thought. Her eyes widened and eyebrows went up. "The break-in. The person who was upstairs. Could that person have been the one who killed her?"

The sisters stared at Angie. Courtney sat back down. "That makes sense. It's possible."

"Why did he break in? What could he have been looking for?" Ellie asked.

"And did he find it?" Jenna made eye contact with Angie. "Or will he be back?"

Angie narrowed her eyes. "If he comes back, then he better be ready for trouble." She would fight and claw anyone who threatened her sisters.

"We need to find out who he is," Ellie said.

"The killer is probably someone from Sweet Cove." Angie was horrified to think that someone from their little, seaside town was capable of murder. "How awful to think a murderer is among us." A chill traveled over her skin. "The killer could be one of my regular customers." The thought made her stomach clench.

Ellie said, "We need to find out why the professor was killed. We need to find out what the intruder was looking for when he broke in here. Then we'll know if it's the same person who committed both crimes."

Jenna said, "Tomorrow, I'll start going through the papers in the upstairs den. I'll check the desk. I'll look around for anything that someone might have an interest in."

"I'll help," Courtney said.

"You and Ellie are returning to Boston tomorrow," Angie said. "You have papers to finish and finals to take and Ellie has to go back to the hotel and give her two weeks notice."

Ellie and Courtney groaned and attempted to protest but Angie cut them off. "I'm not in any danger of getting arrested. I have a few more weeks at the bake shop and then I have to move things out of there. I'll be busy working and then packing things up. Jenna can spend some time looking into the paperwork upstairs. We all have our jobs to do, and then when we finish, we'll all be back here and we can put our heads together about who poisoned the professor and who broke into the house."

"Just don't let anything exciting happen until we get back," Courtney said, trying to lighten the mood.

"Yeah," Ellie agreed. "I've missed everything so far."

Angie grinned. "I'll try not to get arrested until you get back."

Everyone decided to call it a night since the alarm clocks would be going off early the next morning. They climbed the stairs to the second floor and went to their bedrooms. Although, the house was quiet in a matter of minutes, Angie spent a good part of the night tossing and turning with worry.

7

Jenna drove Ellie and Courtney to the train and Angie headed off to the bake shop. The day was overcast with a cool breeze and the gray sky reflected Angie's mood. In the space of a week, she had swung from disheartened about closing her shop and frustrated that she couldn't find somewhere else to move to, and then, jubilant to have been given the gift of the Victorian where not only could she and her sisters live together but she could relocate her café into the house and retain her regular customers.

Now Angie had swung back to worried and unsettled because the professor had been murdered and she was a suspect. She understood why she might be under suspicion, but the whole thing was ridiculous. How would she have had access to the will? How would she even know what was in the professor's will?

Angie unlocked the café door and went inside. Lisa arrived shortly after Angie, and the two started the preparations for the morning customers. Lisa didn't say much as she worked at her tasks. She seemed tired and distracted as she moved about the shop. Her face was pale and puffy, and her usually styled hair looked like it hadn't even been combed today. Angie assumed the cause was the same unsettling reason she herself was feeling subdued.

"How are you doing, Lisa?"

"Shocked." Lisa opened the oven and slid a tray of blueberry muffins onto the wire rack. "I've had a headache since I heard the professor was dead. I just can't talk about it."

Angie didn't ask any more questions and she didn't say anything else to Lisa about the professor. Although, she understood that people processed sad news in different ways, some wanting to talk and others needing to retreat into silence, Angie thought it was better not to keep things bottled up inside for too long.

Once the morning routine was underway and the regulars began to stream in and out of the bake shop, Angie's mood improved. Most of the customers had heard the news that the professor had been murdered and conversations concentrated on speculation about why it happened and who might have done it. Some regulars had heard scuttlebutt that Angie's name was on the list of people to be questioned and they staunchly defended her and proclaimed her innocence. It made Angie happy to be a member of the Sweet Cove community.

Tom sat on his usual counter stool sipping a coffee. "I'll be over around noon on Saturday to look at what you'd like done to the Victorian."

"Noon on Saturday would be great. We'll probably have to do the renovations in parts," Angie said. "We'll have to make the changes as we can afford them."

"No problem with that," Tom told her.

The bake shop door opened and Jenna stepped in, her brown hair in a messy ponytail. She hurried over to the counter stools.

"Hey," she greeted Angie. "I thought I'd stop in for some tea before I tackle the paperwork in the den. I got the girls to the train just in time. They're on their way back to Boston."

Tom's eyes brightened when he saw Jenna come in. "Nice to see you, again."

"You, too, Tom." Jenna gave him a big smile.

"Pull up a stool." Tom indicated the empty stool next to him and Jenna sat down.

Angie brought Jenna a cup of green tea, her favorite. "Tom and I were just talking about the renovations on the house. He's going to come by on the weekend to take a look."

"That's great. It'll be nice to have someone we know and trust to do the work." Jenna lowered her voice and leaned closer to her sister. "What's the town buzz? People know the professor was murdered? That you're a suspect?"

Angie nodded. "Everyone's been very supportive."

"Still can't believe someone would murder the professor." Tom shook his head. "I don't think there's been in a murder in Sweet Cove for decades."

Jenna said, "You heard someone broke into the Victorian?"

"What?" Tom straightened. "When?"

"The night the professor died," Angie said. "I went there in the evening to take care of the cat. I was in the kitchen and heard someone upstairs." A shiver ran down her back recalling the sensation of fear when she heard the person's footsteps on the front staircase. "He ran out. He had been going through the professor's things. There were papers strewn all over the floor of the upstairs den."

"Who the heck would do that?" Tom's usually cheerful face had clouded over.

Angie said, "I think it must be someone from town. The news of the professor's death spread around Sweet Cove by word of mouth that day. It hadn't been reported in any newspapers."

Tom looked steamed. "I don't like the idea that someone from town is up to no good. What's going on? A murder. A break-in."

Angie said, "It's all so unsettling. Who would do it? Who would have anything to gain by breaking into the house? Whoever did it seemed to concentrate his search in the upstairs den. It looked like he was after some kind of paperwork."

"Strange." Tom considered who might have broken into the Victorian. "What kind of paperwork would someone have interest in? I wonder if the intruder is linked to the professor's murder? And who the heck would poison the professor? There aren't many tourists around yet so the killer must be someone from town. We should think about who would have motive."

"Well, Angie would, for one," Jenna kidded. "Since, she inherited the house."

"Not funny." Angie gave Jenna a look.

"You know." Tom stroked his chin absent-mindedly. "I drove past the professor's house that morning, the morning she died. "She was standing on her porch talking to a man. It was that guy who bought this building."

"Davis and Josh Williams bought the building," Angie said.

"It was the older one. The serious one."

Jenna cradled her cup of tea in her hands. "That's Davis Williams, the one who acts like he owns the world. He came to the house last night. He made Angie an offer for the house. Maybe he tried to buy the Victorian from Professor Linden. Maybe she refused."

"Maybe he poisoned her," Tom said. "Professor Linden had no relatives. Maybe Williams thought if he got rid of the professor then he could get his hands on the house." Tom faced Angie. "You better be careful of him."

"Davis Williams couldn't have killed the professor." Angie was gazing off into space. "He wouldn't. Just to try to get her house? Why would a house be so important to him?"

"Well, Angie doesn't have to worry," Jenna told

Tom with a grin on her face. "If Davis Williams ever thought about killing Angie for the Victorian, he'd realize he would never get the house because Angie has relatives. The house would go to me and Ellie and Courtney. So, Angie's safe. At least from Williams."

Angie turned her attention to Jenna, her expression serious. She stared at her sister for a few moments. "I need a will."

"Well, don't go to that new weird-o lawyer. Go to someone else," Tom said.

"There's something about him," Angie said. "There's something subtle. He seems to resent me, that I inherited the Victorian."

"Why would he?" Jenna asked. "He didn't know the professor. He doesn't know you. He's new to Sweet Cove."

"I don't know why. It's just a feeling I get from him."

"Huh," Tom said. "Maybe he killed her."

"Oh, for heaven's sake, Tom," Angie said. "You really have it in for him don't you?" She gave Tom a playful bop on his arm.

Jenna glanced around the bake shop. "It's awful to think the killer is someone from town. It could be someone sitting right in here."

Angie didn't like that one bit. She nervously eyed the customers.

"You're right. Look around," Tom said. "We could come up with a motive for practically everyone in here." He lowered his voice. "There's John Whitman. The professor beat him in the selectman election. He was none too pleased about that. What about votes she cast as selectman? Plenty of people disagreed with her on things, especially her votes that kept people from profiting from building projects the professor squashed. There must be plenty of others who bear a grudge against her."

Angie blew out a sigh. "A grudge so strong it would lead to murder?"

A regular customer, Mrs. Abbott, approached the counter. She was in her eighties, plump, and had bright red hair. "Angie, could you make me one of those energy drinks? The one that has fruit in it?

"I'll get it," Lisa called.

"Um, I'd like Angie to make it," Mrs. Abbott said. She saw the annoyance in Lisa's eyes and told her, "No offense, Lisa. But the one Angie made for me the other day, well, it was something special. I hadn't felt so good for ages."

Angie smiled. "Well, thanks Mrs. Abbott, but I don't think it was because I prepared the drink that it made you feel so good. We all use the same ingredients whenever we make the beverages. I don't do anything special, but I'd be glad to make it for you, if you like."

Mrs. Abbott beamed. "Oh, would you? Thank you so much, Angie."

"I'll ring it up then," Lisa said sullenly. She straightened her apron and scowled at Mrs. Abbott. After giving the woman her change, Lisa grabbed a container of dirty dishes and stomped into the back room to load them into the dishwasher.

As Angie moved down the counter to prepare the drink for the older woman, Tom grinned. "Angie must have a magic touch."

Angie rolled her eyes at him. She mixed the ingredients in a blender, poured the liquid into a take-out cup, and snapped the lid on. Mrs. Abbott was gleeful when Angie handed the drink to her.

Jenna leaned forward to speak to Angie. "What's up with Lisa? She seems so grumpy and out of sorts. You'd think she'd be glad that a customer wants you to prepare a drink, then she doesn't have to do it."

Angie glanced around to see where Lisa was. She lowered her voice. "I know she's been very upset over the professor's death. But I noticed a change in her ever since she found out that I'm going to inherit

Professor Linden's house. She's been acting different, sort of cold and abrupt with me."

"Why would she care if you inherited the house?" Tom asked.

Angie shrugged. "A touch of jealousy? It's understandable. You know, like when someone wins the lottery, people get jealous."

Jenna mused. "Maybe she thinks you'll sell the Victorian and live off the money. She might be worried that you'll close the bake shop and won't re-open it and she'll lose her job."

"But the bake shop is closing in a few weeks and I don't have a new spot to move to yet," Angie said. "She knows all this. She has retirement income from her teaching job. I don't think she needs the money. She just wants to work to keep busy."

"Who knows?" Tom drained his coffee cup. "She's probably upset over the murder. She lives alone. The killer is still at large. She's probably nervous about that."

"Well, I hope she feels better soon." Angie wiped down the counter. "I don't like to see her unhappy."

8

When Angie closed the bake shop for the day, she and Jenna took a bike ride around town and then headed down to Robin's Point, the southernmost end of Sweet Cove where the road followed beside the coastal beaches and cliffs. The point reached out into the sea and years ago, the girls' grandmother owned a small cottage nestled in the dunes next to two other cottages that had been there for over a hundred years. The four sisters and their mother spent many weekends and several weeks each summer staying at Nana's place.

The town of Sweet Cove had rented the land to the cottage owners and, over the years, the lease passed from owner to owner until the town decided that when the most recent leases were up, the cottage owners could purchase their parcels or the town would kick them off the land. The cost of the land was astronomical and the girls' grandmother had no way of buying the property. She decided it would be too costly to buy another parcel of land somewhere else and move the cottage there, so she planned to sell her little house to Sweet Cove for ten thousand dollars. Shortly after the sale went through, the girls' grandmother passed away. Her death was labeled "natural causes" but the family was sure it was from a broken heart.

The town sold the land to the Williams brothers' father, the cottages were knocked down, and ten years later, the Williams brothers constructed a hotel on the point. The architectural design of the resort was in keeping with the quaint flavor of Sweet Cove and the brothers set aside a piece of land on which they created a small public park with access paths down to the town-owned beaches. The brothers hired a management team for the hotel and left the area to oversee other projects in different parts of the country.

Angie had never seen or met the brothers until just the other day. She wondered why they were back. It couldn't be only to buy and refurbish the small building that housed her bake shop.

When the girls reached the park on the point, Jenna and Angie pulled their bikes off the path and sat down on a bench to look out over the Atlantic.

"It's pretty here, but...." Jenna started.

"I know." Angie brushed back a piece of hair that had fallen out of her ponytail. "It will never be the same. We had so much fun here with Nana."

"Let's walk over to the spot." Jenna stood up.

Angie nodded. They left their bikes in the sand and walked along the path. Their nana's former parcel of land now straddled between a section of the park and part of the resort's property. The girls stood on the spot where the cottage used to be and watched the gulls swooping over the rocky coastline. Blue waves crashed against the rocks.

"At least the area where the cottage once stood is open space and not covered over by that thing." Jenna waved her hand towards the resort building. "We can always come and sit where the cottage used to be."

Angie could feel a tingling under her skin as though a low-voltage electric current was running through her body. Every time she visited the place where Nana's cottage used to be, she experienced the same sensation. "Do you feel funny when you stand here?"

Jenna shrugged. "How do you mean?"

"I don't know. I feel ... like something humming through me."

"You mean like emotions? Longing for the past?" Jenna asked.

Angie said, "Yeah. That must be it. I just get a funny feeling when I come back here."

Jenna put her arm through Angie's. They sat on the ground and reminisced about their childhood summers spent on the point and chuckled about silly things they had done.

Jenna breathed out a big sigh. "Everything changes, I guess."

"That's for sure," Angie said, her voice tinged with sadness.

They sat for a few more minutes admiring the view when they heard footsteps approaching behind them. They turned to see Josh Williams coming towards them.

"I thought it was you." He smiled at Angie. "It's a beautiful day."

"Oh. Hi." Angie stood up. Even though she found Josh attractive, Angie wasn't thrilled to see him. It was his and his brother's fault that she was losing her livelihood by not renewing her bake shop's lease. He seemed interested in her, but she knew she could be misinterpreting his intentions. It was kind of a weird and awkward situation. "We're out for a bike ride and stopped for a break. This is my sister, Jenna."

Jenna stood up and shook hands with Josh.

"It's nice to meet you." Josh gave Jenna a pleasant smile and then turned back to Angie. "Would you like to come in to the resort? Have a drink or something to eat?"

"Um, no. But, thanks." Angie was surprised that Josh was inviting them to have a drink with him. "We'll be getting back on the bikes in a minute. We haven't finished our ride."

"We've recently upgraded the resort restaurants. I think they came out great. Maybe you can come by another time. I think you'll like the changes." Josh smiled at Angie. "I'd like your opinion."

Angie's cheeks tinged with pink from Josh's attention. Despite her attraction to him, she couldn't help shake the feeling that he was almost an enemy. She wondered why Josh would want her opinion. "Well, we've never been inside the resort so we don't know what it looked like before."

"You've never been inside?" Josh looked disappointed. "Why, not?

"I...." Angie started to speak but didn't really have an answer.

Jenna said, "We've sort of avoided the resort. Our nana owned one of the original cottages that used to be here on the point. Nana couldn't afford to buy the land, so the town took over her house. Then everything got sold to your family. We used to spend summers here with our nana." She shrugged.

"I'm sorry." Josh seemed sincerely saddened. "It must be hard for you to see the changes."

Angie watched Josh. She was wary of him. Their two families seemed to be at odds. She knew the Williams family wasn't to blame for her nana losing her cottage, but they profited from it and, years later, they were kicking her bake shop out of the building they recently purchased. It seemed that the people in Angie's family were always the ones on the losing end of things. Now the Williams brothers were trying to get their hands on the Victorian. Maybe she was wrong, but money and financial gain seemed to be the overriding motivator in that family. A flood of annoyance shot through her body. They won't get the Victorian from us, no matter how hard they try. Angie attempted to tamp down her feelings, but she was prickling with the injustice of things.

She looked straight at Josh. "We missed you last night."

Josh looked puzzled. "Last night?"

"Your brother paid us a visit. I wondered why you weren't with him."

"Davis visited you? Where?"

"At the Victorian," Angie said.

Josh shook his head. "I didn't know he was going to see you. What did he want?"

Angie cocked her head to one side and raised her eyebrows. I bet you know what he wanted. She put a smile on her face. "Is this the good cop, bad cop routine?"

Josh's forehead scrunched in confusion. "What do you mean?"

Angie said, "You know, one brother plays the bad guy and the other one is the good guy. The good guy gets the victim on his side. Then they both go in for the kill."

Josh's facial muscles tensed and his eyes narrowed. "What did Davis say to you last night?"

"Maybe you should ask him." Angie picked her bike helmet off the ground and Jenna did the same. "You might want to ask him why he didn't tell you what he was up to." Angie started to walk away, but thought of something and stopped. "Your brother was talking to Professor Linden a few minutes before she died. On her porch. Were you there with them as well?"

"What? He was? Are you sure?"

"That's what I heard." Angie wondered if Josh was trustworthy. She wondered if he was playing her, pretending he didn't know what Davis was up to. Thoughts flashed through Angie's mind. Why wouldn't Davis have told Josh that he was making an offer for the Victorian? What was Davis talking to Professor Linden about? Was he pressuring her to sell? Could Davis Williams have poisoned the professor?

"Maybe you need to have a chat with your brother," Angie said over her shoulder as she and Jenna headed off to their bikes.

9

B ecause Professor Linden had no living relatives, she had requested in her will that her body be cremated and buried in a nearby cemetery, and that no formal service should be held. Angie thought it would be important to arrange a gathering of the professor's friends and acquaintances for an informal remembrance reception. She decided that she would host it at the Victorian providing tea, coffee, cold drinks, hot and cold appetizers, and desserts, and that she would invite all of the bake shop's regular customers as well as people the professor knew from town organizations.

When Angie was planning the event, she talked to Tom about it at the bake shop one morning. Tom said, "You know, Angie, the professor's killer may very well show up at the reception. Do you want him in your house? Do you want to take that chance?"

"I thought that might happen," Angie told him. "I intend to be vigilant, watching and listening as I act as host. I wouldn't mind if you were on the lookout too for anything that might seem off."

"I'll keep my eyes and ears open." Tom winked at Angie. "Chief Martin might decide to hire us on as detectives."

"He could do worse," Angie said, smiling.

THE DAY of the reception was warm and sunny and the girls opened the windows to allow a fresh, light breeze to enter the living room and dining room spaces. Ellie and Courtney had come to Sweet Cove for the weekend so all four sisters were on hand to help with the remembrance gathering.

The living room opened to a glassed-in sunroom and there was plenty of room for people to stand, sit and mingle in the first floor rooms and on the wrap-around porch. Angie put out an incredible spread of miniature quiches, savory meatballs in gravy, scalloped potatoes, French bread pizza slices, and a number of different dessert treats. She also created a parfait bar for people to make their own ice cream sundaes with fresh whipped cream and assorted toppings, including the professor's favorite hot fudge sauce from the bake shop.

A few people offered to say a few words telling about the professor's generosity with her time and money to improve and care for the town of Sweet Cove. A framed picture of Professor Linden and a glass vase containing a variety of spring flowers had been placed on a side table. More people than Angie expected congregated in the house to mingle, chat and share reminiscences.

Angie and her sisters moved about the rooms tending to the needs of the guests. When Angie turned around, she saw Josh Williams walking towards her. She had the urge to run away from him, but it was obvious that she had seen him and to try to avoid Josh would have been rude, so she gave him a slight smile and a nod of the head.

Josh's eyes held Angie's as he stepped close to her. "It was very kind of you to have a remembrance for Professor Linden." Even though Angie was trying to be wary of Josh, she couldn't deny the spark of attraction between them.

"Oh, it was the least I could do." Warmth spread

through Angie's body from being so close to Josh. She could smell the fresh scent of his soap. "I'm glad there's such a large turnout."

Josh lowered his voice. "I spoke to my brother about what you told me the other day. It turns out, Davis wanted to buy the Victorian and the reason he hadn't spoken to me about it was because he hoped to purchase it for me as a gift."

"A gift?" Angie's eyes widened in surprise.

Josh nodded. "He was planning to give it to me for my birthday."

"That would have been quite a gift." Angie wondered if Davis really wanted to buy the house for Josh or if he was just telling his brother that to conceal his real reasons. Angie wished she wasn't so suspicious of Davis Williams, but his personality seemed cold and he was hard to read. His manner as a hard-driving businessman was a turnoff.

"It would have been an extremely extravagant gift," Josh said, "but Davis is like that. I know it must be hard to believe, but he can be very sentimental. We only have each other now. Our parents are gone. Davis is very generous to me. He's always thinking of my welfare. That's why he was talking to Professor Linden the day she died. He was asking if she would be amenable to an offer for the house."

"It seems that Davis is a very good brother to you." A twinge of guilt picked at Angie for being so distrustful of Davis.

Josh stepped a bit closer to Angie and her heart did a little flip. "Honestly, I'm glad Davis wasn't able to make the purchase from you. It was excessive and it would have made me uncomfortable, although I do appreciate his attempt to make me happy. I love Victorians, always have. I hope to own one someday."

Angie thought back to running into Josh on Robin's Point near the resort the other day. She felt sheepish about the accusatory tone she had used when telling Josh about Davis' interactions with her when he came to make the offer on the Victorian. Discovering that there was no malicious intent on Davis' part made Angie feel like she had falsely accused him. She wanted to make amends.

"Well, maybe later, if you'd like, I'll give you a tour of the house since you're interested in Victorians," Angie told Josh. "I'm still getting to know it myself. We've only been here a short time and there's so much to the place."

Josh beamed. "I'd love that. Thank you, Angie."

When Josh said her name, she was surprised at the flash of heat that surged through her body and she hoped her reaction wasn't obvious to him. Flustered, Angie wanted to move away from Josh, so she stepped to the side and as she did, she saw Attorney Ford come through the front door. Angie's face took on a worried expression.

"Are you okay?" Josh noticed the abrupt change in Angie's body language and he followed her gaze. "Is something wrong?"

Angie pulled herself together. "No. I'm fine. I'd better see to the refreshments. I'll talk to you later." She took a deep breath as she hurried to the tables to check if the food needed replenishing.

Jenna moved close to Angie. "Did you see who just came in?" she whispered.

"I sure did. I don't know why, but he unnerves me. He always seems like he has something he wants to say to me, but then holds back. See if you can listen in on his conversations. Ask Tom to do the same. I'm going to the kitchen to refill this platter, and try to calm my nerves."

ANGIE RETURNED to the dining room and placed the freshly-filled platter on the table. She glanced around at the guests. Euclid was sitting on top of the dining room cabinet looking none too pleased that his home had been invaded by a group of strangers. The gathering showed no sign of slowing down. People chatted, ate and drank, and groups formed and re-formed as the town residents moved about the large rooms. Angie spotted Betty Hayes, the real estate agent, and crossed the living room to strike up a conversation with her.

"Can I get you anything?" Angie asked.

Betty turned to Angie. "Oh, Angie, no, thanks. Everything's lovely. Well done." She held a dessert plate with a slice of almond cake.

"I'm glad you could come. I'm sure the professor would have appreciated it."

Betty put her hand to her throat. "Oh, that poor woman. Poisoned. Can you imagine?"

Angie said, "It's quite a shock. I keep expecting her to come into the bake shop every morning...." Her voice trailed off. "When did you see the professor last?" Angie knew very well when Betty last saw the professor but she wanted to hear what Betty might say.

"That very morning, the day she died. I saw her at your shop. We had a short chat. It was so busy that day." Betty looked off across the room for a few seconds. "I sat at her table for a few minutes. We talked, just about the usual things, the weather, gardening, the tourist season starting up. Next thing I know, I hear she's dead." Betty looked straight at Angie. "I just couldn't believe it." Betty put a forkful of cake in her mouth.

"Did she seem worried about anything that day?" Angie questioned.

"No." Betty's words were slightly garbled from chewing the bite of cake. "She seemed herself. I was always at her to sell this Victorian. Why on earth would she keep such a thing? It was nonsense for just one person to live in this big house. Anyway, I asked if she was ready to put it on the market. Of course, she said 'no,' so we just talked about what was going on in town, nothing important." Betty looked over at the professor's photograph on the side table and she frowned. "How could this happen in our little town?"

"Did you actively discuss marketing the Victorian for her?"

"My, yes, of course, I did. It's what I do. I am a real estate professional. This house would offer a huge commission. Anyone would want to represent this property. I would be thrilled to be the listing agent. I encouraged the professor to sell, to make her life easier." Betty shook her head. "You know her father lived in Sweet Cove when he was growing up? He left the town and moved to Boston before his mother died."

Angie had no idea why a ripple of tension zinged her stomach when Betty mentioned the professor's father.

Betty went on, "The professor grew up in Boston. She told me that her father was a city man. He didn't like a place like Sweet Cove. There wasn't enough action for him here, not enough stimulation. He couldn't get away from here fast enough, the professor said."

"I didn't know he grew up in town," Angie said.

"Well, he did." Betty took a step closer to Angie and smiled sweetly. "Are you thinking of selling the Victorian, by any chance?"

"No." Angie couldn't help the corners of her mouth turning up at Betty's incessant attempts to list a property. "I'm going to stay here."

Betty's smile fell away and her voice was flat. "Oh."

Angie thought that since Betty knew a good deal

about what went on in town that she might be a good resource for helping to find out who might have poisoned the professor. "Did you ever hear the professor arguing with anyone? I wonder why someone would kill her. What motive could someone possibly have?"

"Sometimes she'd have disagreements with people. Being a town selectman, that's to be expected, though. But none of that is reason to kill someone."

"Did you ever hear of any threats made to her?" Angie wondered if Betty might have heard some gossip since she worked with so many people in town.

"No. My, goodness. Threats?" Betty frowned.

"Well, someone wasn't happy with her," Angie said.

Betty spoke in a hushed tone. "What do you think of that new lawyer?"

Angie stiffened. "Why do you ask?"

"He seems very stuffy, if you want my opinion, and not very pleasant either. How will he ever attract business with that personality?" Betty eyed him standing on the other side of the room.

"Have you had dealings with him?" Angie hoped Betty had some information about him.

"Not directly. I will, soon, no doubt, as people will use him for their real estate closings." She made a face. "I wish there was another lawyer in town. He just seems so...odd." Betty licked the fork in her hand. "Did you make this cake? It's delicious. I've never had almond cake that tasted so good."

Angie was about to answer when Betty said, "The professor didn't like him either."

Angie's eyebrows went up. "The lawyer? She didn't like him? Why, not?" A strange sensation fluttered through Angie's body.

"She went to him for something or other. She said he didn't seem too eager to help her." Betty scraped the last cake crumbs from her plate.

"Help her with what?"

"Oh, look." Betty turned her attention to the foyer. "There's Davis Williams. I need to speak with him."

"Betty." Angie put her hand on Betty's arm. "What did the professor go to the lawyer for?"

"Hmmm...." It was clear that Betty was ready to put her claws into Davis Williams. "Oh. Um. I don't recall." She handed Angie the dirty plate and fork.

"Think back on it, would you?" Angie asked. "Was it recently that the professor went to see Jack Ford?"

"About a month ago, I'd say." Betty rubbed her chin. "I think it was something about her father."

"The professor's father? Why?"

"I think so. Yes. I can't remember about what though. Maybe she never told me." Betty watched Davis Williams enter the dining room. "I'll talk to you later, Angie. I have some business to discuss with Davis." She made a beeline for Williams.

Jenna and Tom came over to Angie.

"Well, someone's lost in thought," Tom said.

Angie jumped. "I didn't hear you come up." She leaned in towards Tom and her sister and told them what Betty had just said about Jack Ford and the professor.

"That's strange," Jenna said. "What would the professor have to ask about her father?"

"How would Ford know anything about the professor's father?" Tom glanced over at Ford. "Her father must have died like fifty years ago."

Jenna followed Tom's gaze. "Maybe Betty's confused about what the professor said. Maybe she heard it wrong."

"I don't know." Angie had a faraway look in her eyes.

"Angie?" Jenna said.

Angie blinked. "Where's Euclid?"

Tom looked puzzled. "Why do you want the cat?"

Angie turned for the dining room just as Jenna said, "Last I saw, he was on top of the China cabinet."

Angie left the living room, crossed the foyer, and walked into the dining room. Courtney came up to Angie and said, "Here, let me take that plate from you."

"What?" Angie asked. "Oh, yeah, thanks." She handed Betty's used plate and fork to Courtney.

Angie looked up at Euclid who was sitting on the cabinet glaring at everyone. The cat shifted its attention to Angie. Angie had a strange feeling run through her body when she was talking to Betty about the professor. Something made her want to find Euclid, but now standing there looking up at him, she had no idea what she wanted. Angie shook herself.

Courtney came into the room carrying a stack of clean plates and as she passed Angie, she paused and said, "You okay? You've got a weird look on your face."

Angie forced a smile. "I just wanted to be sure Euclid was behaving." She reached out. "Here let me help you with those dishes."

LATE AFTERNOON LIGHT filtered in through the Victorian's windows as people began to head home from the reception. Ellie stood in the living room excitedly explaining to several people the plans for the bed and breakfast. Jenna was talking with a woman from Sweet Cove who ran a gift shop down by the point. The woman was interested in carrying some of Jenna's jewelry line and she was arranging an appointment to view some of the pieces. Courtney and Angie carried trays of dishes and glasses into the kitchen and set them on the table to wait until the latest dishwasher load had finished.

"Woo," Courtney let out a breath as she leaned against the kitchen counter. "That was a lot of work. I should have stayed at school and let you do everything," she joked.

"Thanks for your help. You're a hard worker." Angie hugged her sister. "It was a very nice remembrance for the professor. I'm glad we did it."

"You were very kind to plan it." A man's voice spoke and the girls spun around surprised to see Josh Williams standing in the kitchen.

"Josh." Angie crossed the space to him. "Can we get you something?"

Josh was about to speak, when Angie remembered her promise to give him a tour of the Victorian. "Oh. The tour. Come in." She stretched her arms out indicating the dirty dishes and pots and pans that covered almost all of the counter space. "So, this is the kitchen." She chuckled. "A huge mess."

Josh laughed. "It's great."

"Not the best time to see this room." Angie placed her hand on his upper arm to steer him out of the disaster area. His solid biceps were evident beneath her fingers and her breath caught in her throat. She had to swallow hard before she spoke again. "I'll show you the parts of the house that don't look like a hurricane just blew through them."

"The kitchen doesn't always look like this?" Josh teased.

Courtney called after them. "Don't let Angie fool you. It does always look like this."

The dishwasher beeped to indicate the latest washing cycle had completed. Courtney sighed wondering how everyone else managed to be absent when it was time to unload and load the dishwasher.

ANGIE SHOWED Josh the music room, the sunroom, the library, a den, and then returned to the living room. He commented on the layout of the home, the antiques and other furnishings and told Angie how lucky she was to be able to live in the Victorian.

"I'll show you the second floor." Angie led him into the foyer and was about to start up the stairs, when Jenna called to her that her phone was ringing. Courtney hurried over to her sister to hand her the cell phone.

Angie answered and her face went pale. "Yes." She listened and then said, "Yes, that would be fine. I understand." She clicked off and stared down at the phone for several seconds.

Jenna noticed the expression of distress on Angie's face. "Who was that? What's wrong?"

Angie sighed. "It was a Detective Matthews. I have an appointment with him tomorrow. He wants to discuss Professor Linden's death with me."

No one spoke for a moment, and then Jenna stepped close to her sister and put her hand on Angie's shoulder. "It'll be okay."

"I'll go to the police station with you," Courtney said.

Angie gave a slight shake of her head. "No. Tomorrow's Monday. You and Ellie need to head back to Boston early in the morning. I'm just going to talk with him. That's all." She smiled trying to reassure her sisters, but she had to blink back some tears that were threatening to fall. She tried to joke when she told them, "He isn't going to throw me in prison tomorrow."

Angie's heart sank. I hope he isn't, anyway.

10

Early the next morning, Jenna went to the bake shop to help Lisa with the early morning rush so that Angie could head for the police station to keep her appointment with the detective. As Angie climbed the steps and approached the front door of the station, her knees were shaking and her legs wobbled. She chastised herself for feeling so queasy and nervous. She was innocent, but acting so unsure and afraid would not convince any law enforcement officer that she had nothing to do with Professor Linden's death.

Walking into the tiny lobby, Angie forced herself to push her shoulders back and straighten her posture. She approached the front desk and asked for Detective Matthews in a clear, loud voice. Almost too loud, since the receptionist looked like she wondered why Angie was shouting.

Angie cleared her throat and lowered her volume. "I'm Angie Roseland. I have an appointment with the detective."

Angie turned towards the sound of footsteps coming down the hall. The man was tall, about Angie's age, with broad shoulders and a determined manner. "Miss Roseland? I'm Detective Matthews."

"Nice to meet you. Please call me Angie."

They shook and the detective ushered Angie into a small conference room off the main hallway. The room was plain and harshly lit and a scratched, plastic table and two old, wooden chairs sat in the center of the space. The detective indicated with his hand that Angie should take one of the chairs. The detective sat opposite her across the table.

"So, Miss Roseland. Angie." He pushed a button on a tape recorder that was sitting in the middle of the table. "Detective Ron Matthews is speaking with Angela Roseland." He stated the date, time and place of the interview.

"Would you state your name and address, please."

Angie did. She tried to take even breaths to calm her hammering heart and skittering nerves.

"What is your occupation?" The detective's pen was poised over a page of his notebook.

"I own the Sweet Dreams Bake Shop. I work there every day. Until around 3pm. Sometimes I'm there later getting ready for the next morning."

"Do you work there alone?"

"I have an employee, Lisa Barrows. And often my sisters help out."

"How long have you had the store?"

"Only a year. The building has new owners now, so I have to vacate the premises in a couple of weeks. The new owners will be replacing the space with something else."

"Will you be moving the business to another location in Sweet Cove?"

"I don't have firm plans as of yet." Angie thought it best not to talk about moving the shop to the Victorian.

"Did you attend college?"

"Yes, I went to MIT. I have a degree in chemistry."

The detective's eyebrows went up. "Chemistry?" He leveled his eyes at Angie. "You're aware, Miss Roseland, that Professor Linden was poisoned?"

Angie nodded, her face was serious. "Chief Martin told me."

The detective leaned slightly forward. "Did he tell you what was used to poison her?"

Angie shook her head. "No. He didn't." Under her shirt, a bead of sweat rolled down her back.

Detective Matthews narrowed his eyes. "Since you majored in chemistry, would you like to have a guess what was found in Professor Linden's body?"

"I would not." Angie met the detective's eyes. "I didn't study how to poison people."

"It's interesting that Professor Linden died shortly after leaving your shop." The detective leaned back in his chair. "Who made her beverages that day?"

"I was the one who made the professor's first coffees of the day. She always requested that I make them." Angie was quiet for a few moments. "I'm not sure who made her other drink though." She thought back to the day. "The professor always had the same thing every morning. She would sit at one of the tables and have a bakery item and a mocha latte. Some of the regulars would sit at her table and talk. They'd come and go. She might read the paper for a little while or a book she brought with her. She'd stay for about an hour and then when she was ready to leave, she always had a hazelnut latte to go." Angie's eyebrows knitted together as she pondered the last morning that the professor was in the bake shop. "I don't know. I don't know who made the take-out drink."

The detective sighed. "Who was working that day?"

"Me. Lisa. My sister, Courtney. She's a senior in college. She came up for the weekend." Angie folded her hands and rested them on the table. "It doesn't really matter who made the drinks. Lots of people could have accessed them. People sat with the professor at her table to talk with her. Just about anyone could have slipped something into her drink."

"Professor Linden left her Victorian home to you in her will, along with a substantial amount of money."

Angie nodded.

The detective frowned. "Why did she?"

Angie let out a sigh. She didn't like the detective's accusatory tone. "I have no idea."

Detective Matthews continued. "You aren't related. You weren't long time friends."

"No. The inheritance was as much a surprise to me as it is to you, Detective."

He drummed his fingers on the table. "And when did you know you were in Professor Linden's will?

"When Attorney Jack Ford told me. After Professor Linden passed away."

"You stood to gain from her death." The detective's tone of voice was harsh.

Angie looked across the room, not focusing on anything, just gazing into space.

The detective was about to speak when Angie turned back to him. She placed her hands in her lap, and said softly, "No one gains from someone's death, Detective."

Angie and the detective sat in silence for a few moments, the ticking of the wall clock the only sound in the room.

"Is there anything else? If not, I need to get to work." Angie didn't wait for an answer. She stood up, walked to the door, and left the detective sitting alone in the room.

"How did it go?" Jenna rushed from behind the counter when she saw her sister come into the bake shop. "I've been so worried."

Angie took her jacket off and replaced it with her apron. "He just asked me questions."

Tom was sitting in his usual spot at the counter. "You okay, Angie?"

She smiled at him. "Yeah, I am, now that I'm back here."

One of her regular customers hurried over. "Angie. I've been waiting for you. Will you make me one of those energy drinks?"

"Of course," Angie said. "Pick out the flavor you'd like."

"Angie!" A local called to her and he lifted his cup indicating the need for a refill.

Angie nodded and turned to get the coffee pot, but before she did, she looked back to Tom. "Just another day at the bake shop." Her eyes twinkled.

When the morning rush slowed, Jenna brought Angie a cup of tea. "Tell me what happened at the police station. Are they going to leave you alone now?"

Angie sipped from the mug and leaned against the cabinet. "I don't know. They can't pin the professor's death on me. Where's the proof?"

Jenna breathed out. "Thank heavens." She squeezed Angie's arm.

With her tea mug in one hand, Angie opened the cooler to see what needed replenishing. "I'm not worried. Well, not too much, anyway. I wouldn't be surprised if the detective calls Courtney and Lisa in for questioning. He was very interested to know who made the professor's drinks the day she was murdered."

Jenna groaned. "Why don't they hunt down the actual killer and leave innocent people alone?"

"Someone in this town murdered Professor Linden," Angie said. "Why?" She put her mug down. "I hope the police don't just keep barking up the wrong trees. We need to think about this, Jenna. Someone was in our house. What was he looking for? Is the person who was in our house the same person who killed the professor?"

Jenna said, "I haven't found anything in the upstairs den that someone would be interested in. What was he looking for? What did he want?"

Angie wiped down the preparation counter. "We need to focus on the motive for killing the professor. It was premeditated. Someone planned it. The killer had to get the poison and plot to put it into the professor's coffee." Angie stopped cleaning and tapped her finger against her cheek, thinking. "It has to be someone who knew her, knew her routine. I need to talk to Lisa and Courtney about who was in the shop when the professor was here that day. That way we can narrow down the suspects."

"And then," Jenna said, "we can figure out which one of those people had motive."

"I'll talk to Lisa before she leaves today," Angie said.

"Good," Jenna said. "I'll call Courtney later this afternoon. Then tonight we'll put together a master list of suspects and figure out who might have had reason to poison the professor."

11

Just before 3pm, Angie asked Lisa if she'd stay for a few minutes to talk about the day the professor was poisoned.

Lisa was putting her apron into the laundry bin. "I guess I could, but only for a few minutes. I have a job interview. Since you'll be closing the bake shop, I'd like to find something soon."

Angie's eyebrows went up. "That's great. Where are you interviewing?"

"At the resort. They're looking for a receptionist who can also sometimes act as a reservation specialist. I've never done that, but I think I could learn it pretty fast."

"Good luck. I hope it works out."

They sat down at one of the café tables. Angie opened a notebook.

"What do you want to talk about?" Lisa asked. Her brows knitted together.

"I thought we could think about who was in the shop the morning the professor was killed. Make a list." Angie pulled a pen from her apron.

"Why?"

"To try to figure out who did it," Angie said.

"Won't the police do that?"

"I think it will help the police. I had to speak with a detective this morning. I think he'll probably want to question you and Courtney."

A look of worry washed over Lisa's face. "But we didn't have anything to do with the death." Lisa's eyes got watery.

"Don't worry. The detective just asked simple questions, straight forward stuff. Just tell him what you remember. He's just trying to gather information." Angie thought it best that she leave out the part about how the detective's interrogation made her feel nervous and uncomfortable.

Lisa clutched her hands together.

"It'll be okay." Angie gave her a comforting smile. "Let's think who was here the morning of the murder."

Angie started making a list. "Police Chief Martin was here and Patrolman Talbot. The professor, of course. You, me, and Courtney. Tom." Angie wrote the names on the pad of paper. She looked at Lisa. "Who else?"

"The real estate agent, Betty Hayes." Lisa rubbed her temple.

"Oh," Angie said. "Davis and Josh Williams were here that day. They came in to check out the shop for the renovations they have planned."

"Mrs. Abbott," Lisa said. "That group of older men who come in every morning. And, Selectman Johnson."

They went on for a few more minutes adding names to the list. Lisa checked her watch. "I need to go now. I don't want to be late for my interview."

"Oh, right. Thanks. If you think of anyone else, let me know tomorrow." Angie put her pen down. She wanted to say something to Lisa that might help her to worry less. "You know, I don't think the murder was random. I think someone specifically wanted the professor dead. I know the killer hasn't been caught, but I don't think any of us are in danger."

Lisa seemed to consider what Angie said. She nodded.

"Thanks for helping me with the list." Angie smiled at her. "Good luck with the interview."

Lisa gathered her things. "Thanks."

Angie felt badly that closing the bake shop was probably contributing to Lisa's distress. She sighed, picked up her notebook, and placed it in her purse.

AFTER DINNER, Angie and Jenna sat in the living room going over the list of people who had visited the bake shop on the day that Professor Linden was poisoned.

"I talked to Courtney on the phone this afternoon." Jenna held a piece of paper with names written on it. "What she said matches up with the names you wrote down."

"That's everyone then. These are the people who had access to the professor's drinks." Angie thought of something. "But what about after the professor left the bake shop. She could have stopped to talk to someone on her way home."

"Tom said that Davis Williams was talking to the professor on her front porch shortly before she died." Jenna put her list of names on the coffee table. "She had her take-out latte with her, but I don't see how Williams could slip poison into her cup. Unless she opened it while she was standing on her porch."

"Doesn't seem likely," Angie said. "The poison couldn't take effect that fast, could it?"

"I suppose not." Jenna tapped her pencil against her thigh. "Should we cross off Davis Williams from the suspect list?"

"Did he get near the professor in the shop that morning? I'm just thinking out loud, I know you weren't there." Angie stood and started pacing around the room. "I don't think he did, but I can't be sure. Wait. He and Josh went into the back room for a while. I guess he could have accessed the professor's takeout latte as he walked past the counter. We were all busy. We might not have noticed if he tampered with her drink." Angie ran her hand through her hair. "Let's keep him on the list for now."

Jenna picked the list off the coffee table and looked it over again. "What about what you told me that Betty said about the professor going to see that new lawyer. Betty said the professor asked the lawyer something about her father."

Angie sat down. "Yeah. That's strange, isn't it? The professor's father is long dead. What could she want the lawyer for? How would Ford know anything about Professor Linden's father?"

"Betty might have gotten it wrong. She can be a scatterbrain."

"That's for sure." Angie rolled her eyes. "Betty hasn't been any help finding me a new location for the bake shop."

"If you weren't going to move the shop here, then you'd have to find a new Realtor." Jenna stretched. "Let's go make some hot tea."

When the girls stood up and headed for the kitchen, Euclid rose from his spot on the sofa and arched his back in a mighty stretch. He jumped down and followed Angie and Jenna. Angie took out mugs and milk and set them on the table. Jenna filled the kettle and placed it on the burner. They sat at the kitchen table while they waited for the water to boil. Euclid leaped up onto the counter and then jumped to the top of the fridge where he perched.

Angie fiddled with her mug. "I don't have a lot of money saved. I'm nervous about how long it will take to get the money from the estate. When the bake shop closes in a couple of weeks, then I won't have any income."

"Oh. I didn't think of that." Jenna's brow furrowed.

"I won't be able to afford the renovations without the inheritance. It will take two or three months to get that money. Once I get it, it will probably take Tom a few weeks to complete the changes that I need to open the shop. The summer will be over by then. I'll miss all of that business."

"You'll be living here as caretaker until you get the money, so it won't cost you anything. The estate will pay the utilities and that portion of the taxes. That will save you something," Jenna said.

"Maybe we can get the bed and breakfast going for the summer months," Angie said. "Ellie can get a website up and running to advertise and take reservations. I think Ellie and I can get things ready in time to take guests. I just worry about the bake shop being closed so long. My customers might not return when I finally do open."

The tea kettle whistled and Jenna picked it up and poured the water into the mugs. She said, "We need to make a budget. Then we can figure out what we all need to contribute towards the household costs. There isn't a mortgage to pay and none of us will have to pay rent anymore. You don't need to have an income over the summer. It'll work out with all of us pitching in."

Angie nodded and raised her mug. "Here's to helping each other."

Just as Jenna smiled and clinked her mug against Angie's, the front doorbell rang. Euclid startled. He opened his mouth wide and let out a hiss.

Jenna glanced at the clock on the stove. "It's late. Someone's ringing the doorbell?"

"Who could it be?" Angie stood and started out of the kitchen with Jenna right behind her.

"Stay here, Euclid." Jenna shut the kitchen door to keep the cat from following them to the foyer.

Angie opened the front door. Lisa Barrows, Angie's employee, stood on the porch, clutching a paper bag, her face scrunched with worry.

12

"Lisa." Of all the people who could have been at the door, Lisa was the last person Angie expected to see. "Are you, okay? Come in."

Lisa's eyes were red and her shoulders slightly hunched. Her eyes flicked from Angie to Jenna and back. "I...." She clutched the paper bag to her chest.

"Come sit down." Angie gestured to the living room.

"Can we get you a drink?" Jenna asked.

"No, no." Lisa pushed the paper bag at Angie. "I'm quitting. Here are my uniform shirts."

Angie blinked in surprise. "What? Why?"

"I got the job at the resort. I want to start right

away." Lisa shifted her weight from foot to foot. "I'm sorry for the short notice."

Short notice? This is no notice. "We're only open for two more weeks. Won't the resort let you give a two-week notice?" Angie didn't know how she could run the bake shop without Lisa's help and she was certain she wouldn't be able to hire someone for the remaining two weeks. The high school girls who helped out in the shop in the afternoons wouldn't be able to take up the slack either since it was the end of April and they were still in school.

"The resort would let me give notice, but...." Lisa's voice shook.

"But, what?" Angie wondered why Lisa was in such a hurry to leave the bake shop.

"I don't want to work there anymore. I'm sorry." Lisa's cheeks were bright red.

"Did I do something to upset you?" Angie asked.

Euclid was howling in the kitchen demanding to be let out.

"Why don't we sit down?" Jenna hoped that by sitting together they could sort out why Lisa wanted to leave without giving any notice.

Lisa shook her head. "No, you didn't do anything. I just can't work there any more. I have to go." She edged towards the door.

"Lisa, tell me what's wrong." Angie gently put her hand on Lisa's arm.

"You didn't do anything. I just don't want to work there. It upsets me. The professor's death...well, I...it scares me. I don't want to work in the place where she got poisoned." Lisa's eyes started to get all watery.

Angie could almost feel Lisa's distress, it was so palpable. "Is there something I can do to make it easier? To make you feel less upset? We don't know for sure that the professor was poisoned in the bake shop."

Lisa took a step back. She shook her head. "I need a change. I'm sorry, Angie." She whirled and left the Victorian, shutting the door with a bang.

Jenna stood with her mouth open. Euclid was still wailing.

"What the heck? Now what will I do?" Angie rubbed her neck. "Lisa is so upset. She must be superstitious or something." She looked down the hall to the kitchen and called out, "Jeez, Euclid, stop that screeching."

"I'll let him out." Jenna walked back to the kitchen. Angie followed. Jenna opened the door and Euclid shot down the hall like he was blown from a cannon.

Angie watched him fly past her. "Sheesh."

The girls sat at the kitchen table.

Angie said, "Lisa's mother passed away last year. I wonder if the professor's death is even harder on Lisa because she suffered a loss not long ago."

"That could be. Maybe being in the shop is too hard because it brings up sad feelings and reminds her of the loss of her mother."

"I feel bad for her." Angie rested her chin in her hand and placed her elbow on the table. "I also feel bad that now I'm without an employee and I can't run the place alone."

"I'll help out at the shop," Jenna said. "I've helped plenty of times. I know what to do. I'm not as quick as Lisa, but I can manage."

"But, your jewelry. You can't take time from your business." Angie's face was drawn. She lifted her mug to her lips but it was empty.

"Sure I can. The bake shop is pretty much done by 3pm. I'll work on the jewelry after I finish at the shop."

Angie lifted her eyes. "Really? I can help you put your designs together in the evening. We can do it. We'll run the two businesses together." She gave an uneasy smile. "That is, if we don't collapse from exhaustion first."

Jenna chuckled. "I never thought I'd say this, but thank heavens it's only two weeks before your shop closes."

13

Every time Angie walked down Elm Street she couldn't help but admire the beautiful homes that lined both sides of the road. It was an historic district of Sweet Cove and many of the homes were built in the 1600s to 1700s. Some were in the Federal style and others were Georgian Colonial mansions. Mature trees grew along the sidewalks and in the summer the branches and leaves created a canopy over the road.

A small brass plaque on a brick and brownstone house said, "Jack Ford, Attorney at Law." Angie climbed the stairs, opened the heavy, glossy black door, and entered a small waiting room decorated with period furniture. There was a large wooden reception desk to the left, but no one was there to welcome any clients who might come in. It was after five in the afternoon and Angie wondered if the receptionist might have left for the day.

Angie had made an appointment to have a will drawn up and even though Tom told her not to use Jack Ford, he was the only lawyer in Sweet Cove. She didn't want to have to go to another town for something that seemed so simple to put together.

Angie sat down on a small, camelback sofa assuming that Mr. Ford would come out from his office when he was free. While leafing through a magazine, she heard Jack Ford's voice but couldn't make out what he was saying. She thought he might be calling to her to come into his office, so she walked over to the open door and popped her head in. He wasn't behind his desk. Angie started to back out when she heard Attorney Ford speaking from a room to the rear of his office. It seemed he was on the phone.

"I told you, I couldn't find it." His voice was firm. "She came in while I was up there."

Angie froze.

"I didn't have enough time. I had to turn the lights off fast. I couldn't very well stay there searching in the dark with her in the house."

A cold chill rushed through her veins. What's he

talking about? Was he the one that broke into the Victorian?

"I told you. I'll take care of it."

Angie ran to the sofa and sat. She lifted the magazine in front of her face with trembling fingers. She wanted to run from the building, but she didn't want to indicate to Ford that she'd heard his conversation.

Footsteps could be heard crossing his office space and he appeared in the doorway. Ford startled when he saw Angie sitting there in the waiting room. Angie lowered her magazine.

"Miss Roseland?" Ford had a questioning look on his face.

"Hello." Angie tried to keep her voice even and steady.

"I thought your appointment was tomorrow." He moved to the receptionist's desk to look at the appointment ledger.

Angie said, "Oh, is it? I thought it was today. I'm sorry." Here was an excuse for Angie to flee and she made a move to get up.

"Oh," Jack Ford said. "My mistake. It is today. I hope you haven't been waiting long."

"Oh, no. I just arrived a second ago." Angie didn't want him to think she'd been in the waiting room long enough for her to hear his phone discussion.

"Well, please, come in." Ford gestured to his office.

She put the magazine down and stood straight. Turning to pick up her purse, she took a deep breath to steady herself. Angie faced Attorney Ford determined not to show any signs of unease.

She plastered a fake smile on her face and said, "Yes. Thank you. I'm looking forward to working with you," she lied. She entered his office first and sat in one of the chairs placed in front of his desk. As Ford walked around to take his seat, Angie thought of the saying, "Keep your friends close, and your enemies closer."

Indeed.

"So," Ford said. "You'd like to have a will drawn up." He took some papers from a leather folder.

"Yes. I think it's necessary. Even though I'm young, well, one never knows." Angie gave Ford a pointed look. "Now that I have assets, I want to make sure that they're protected." Why the heck did you break into the Victorian? "I have three sisters and if anything should happen to me, I want them taken care of."

"Of course." Ford pulled a silver pen from his drawer.

Angie said, "One can never be too careful, can one?" I'll get to the bottom of this. I'm watching you, Ford.

"A will is really a simple legal matter. I'll go over some questions with you and then I'll draw it up and have you return next week to sign it. I'll keep it here in the safe. Just let your loved ones know that I prepared it. Should they ever need it, they'll know to contact me."

"I'd like two originals prepared," Angie told him. "You may keep one here on file. I'll keep the other one." Her voice showed no sign of weakness.

Something passed fleetingly over Ford's face and he hesitated for a beat. Then he said, "Of course. Whatever, you wish."

WHEN ANGIE FINISHED WITH FORD, she couldn't race home fast enough to tell Jenna what she overheard him saying on the phone.

They sat at the dining room table. Jenna's face was flushed. "Him? Ford? The attorney? He was in here? How dare he?" She stood up and started pacing. "Why? What does he want?"

"Well, I can't be sure he was the one who broke in, but he said on the phone that he didn't have time to find it. Whatever 'it' is. So if he was the one who was in here, then it must still be in the house."

"He'll be back then," Jenna said. "Should we tell the police what you heard him say?"

"I don't know." Angie crossed her arms and leaned on the tabletop. "What I heard doesn't mean anything. It doesn't implicate Ford. He could just brush off what I heard. He could say he was talking about something else. There's no evidence. I just overheard a conversation."

"Ugh." Jenna groaned. "I guess you're right. There really isn't anything to take to the police. But we better be careful of him."

14

After closing the bake shop for the day, Angie walked the two miles to Betty Hayes' real estate office. It was a hectic morning without Lisa Barrows to help, but Jenna rose to the occasion and they fell into a rhythm of baking and serving the customers.

Angie and Jenna were both worn out when they locked the shop's door for the day. Jenna headed back to the Victorian to take a shower and a nap and then she would begin working on new designs and assembling jewelry for her internet orders. Angie was going to stop at the grocery store after her meeting with Betty Hayes, and would make dinner later in the day so that Jenna could continue working. Angie planned to help Jenna with jewelry assembly in the evening. They had long days ahead of them, but they were determined to get through the next two weeks successfully.

Betty's office was a two-room wing attached to her main house. The areas around the structures were beautifully landscaped with different plants blooming throughout the seasons. Even in winter, the grounds looked striking with various greens and red berries adding color to the cold, quiet landscape. Angie followed the brick pathway to ring the office's doorbell and she noticed forsythia and crocuses and tulips in bloom around the yard.

Betty opened the door before Angie reached the steps.

"Hello, Angie. You're right on time." Betty held the door open for Angie to enter. They sat at an old, round, oak table tucked in the corner of the room next to floor to ceiling windows that looked out over the gardens.

"I love spring," Angie said. "Your garden is coming to life."

"It's a bit later this year," Betty noted. "It was a harsh winter."

"You must enjoy seeing all the plants blooming." Angie gazed out the window at the flowers.

"Oh yes. I learned to garden from my grand-mother. We'd spend hours together tending the plants. I have a small greenhouse in back. Other-wise, I'd go crazy during the winter without flowers and plants." Betty opened a folder and pulled out some papers. "Here is the agreement. It covers the next sixty days. I'm confident I'll be able to find you a location for your shop in that time. You just have to sign here." Betty handed Angie a pen and pointed to the line where she was to sign her name.

"I've decided not to renew our agreement." Angie put the pen on the table.

Betty's lips puckered in a pout. "No? Why on earth not? You need to find a place for your business."

"I might move the shop to the Victorian. The necessary remodel wouldn't be done until after the summer, but I think it's the best option."

"I don't know, Angie. Is that wise? You're putting all your eggs in one basket."

"I think it will work out."

"Do you think it's a good idea to keep that old place?" Betty leaned forward, a fake caring smile on her lips. "You're young. Why be tied to such a money pit? It will suck you dry having to maintain that old thing." She cocked her head. "Think of how wealthy you'd be if you sold it. You wouldn't have to work again for a long time. Invest the profit well and you could live off the interest indefinitely."

Angie narrowed her eyes. "You're the second person who's said that to me recently."

Betty ignored the comment. "Think of it. You could travel. Live somewhere warm in the winter. You're young. Enjoy yourself. Don't lock yourself to that old, dark place."

Angie didn't respond. She knew that Betty was only concerned with her own interests and what would benefit her pocketbook and selling the Victorian would provide a massive agent's commission. Angie chuckled inwardly at the way Betty expressed such concern over Angie's well-being. Artificial concern.

"Oh, I know it's all very new and exciting. But you'll tire of that place and all of its problems very soon." Betty put the agreement back in the folder and closed it. "When you're ready, you know where to find me." She smiled sweetly at Angie.

Angie didn't appreciate the unsolicited advice or Betty's blatant phoniness when money was involved, but she forced a smile and said, "I'll let you know if I ever decide to sell."

Betty clasped her hands together. "Very good. Remember, spring is an excellent time to put property on the market."

"I'll remember." Angie was about to leave but thought of something. "Did you recall what Professor Linden asked the lawyer to do for her? You mentioned it at the reception. It was regarding her father, you said."

Betty blinked several times and then she recalled the conversation she'd had with Angie. "I don't think the professor ever elaborated. I don't know."

"Did the professor ever show interest in selling the Victorian?"

"Once she did, not too long ago, but it was fleeting." Betty said more to herself than to Angie, "I should have pounced on it when I had the chance."

"What did you say?" Angie asked.

Betty waved her hand. "Oh, nothing. Can't look to the past. Must focus on the future."

"Did the professor ever mention Davis Williams to you, that he made an offer on the Victorian?"

"Davis? I don't think so." Betty smiled. "Why all the questions? Are you a detective now, Angie?" She chuckled just as a knock sounded on the door. "Oh, my next appointment is here. Remember what I said about the Victorian. You give it some thought. I'd be glad to help you get that place off your hands."

Betty rose from her seat and Angie did the same. Angie nodded, but she was not selling the house.

Angie was deep in thought as she turned the corner to Main Street and nearly collided with Josh Williams.

"Josh. Sorry. I was thinking about something and wasn't paying attention."

"Angie. It's nice to see you. How are you doing?" His blue eyes warmed her.

"I'm okay." Still annoyed with Betty, she managed a slight smile.

"Thanks again for your hospitality hosting Professor Linden's remembrance reception. And thanks for the tour. The house is great." Josh walked in step with Angie. "Did you meet with the detective? Did it go okay?"

Angie thought how sincere Josh seemed in his questions and she contrasted that with the selfish interest that Betty had shown. Walking along the sidewalk with Josh, Angie could feel her muscles relaxing. Her meeting with Betty had stressed her and she hadn't realized how tense she'd been feeling. "I met with the detective the other day. He is a very suspicious person."

Josh chuckled. "I guess he has to be in his line of work. In his eyes, it must always be guilty until proven innocent."

Angie smiled. "I'm glad I don't have to be so negative in my line of work."

"You're the complete opposite of that. Your job requires a very specific set of skills."

"Does it? What are they?" Angie eyed Josh.

"Well." Josh stopped walking. Angie turned to see why he stopped. "Are you in a hurry? This is a nice pub." Josh indicated the building next to them. "If you'd like a coffee or a glass of wine, I can explain the importance of your skill set for being a bake shop owner." Josh had a twinkle in his eyes.

Warmth spread through Angie's body like molasses, slow and easy, taking its time to heat up every part of her. She almost felt the tingle of a blush coloring her cheeks. Angie was about to tell Josh that she had to get to the market and then hurry home to make dinner, but she was tired of being overworked and rushed, and one quick drink wouldn't take much time. She wanted to accept Josh's offer, even if he and his brother were part of the reasons why she was feeling harried. "A glass of wine sounds nice," Angie said.

A look of surprise flickered over Josh's face and was quickly replaced with a smile that lit him up. "Really? Well, great." He stepped to the pub's entrance and opened the door for Angie.

They took seats by the window and each had a glass of merlot.

"So. Tell me about my skill set." Angie took a sip from her glass.

"There are very important characteristics needed to own a café." Josh crossed his arms on the table top and leaned forward. "A café owner has to be part chemist, part psychologist, part excellent listener, part skilled advice giver, and part savvy businessperson."

Angie locked eyes with Josh. "Hmm...."

"Also, the café owner has to have a warm and friendly personality so that customers feel welcome."

"You've given this a lot of thought, I see," Angie teased. "I'm not sure about a lot of things on that list. I think I might need to work on some of them."

Josh cocked his head. "Which ones do you have mastered?"

"Well, the chemist part, for one."

"That's how you make such excellent desserts. How do you know so much about chemistry?"

Sitting across from Josh, Angie was thinking about a different kind of chemistry. "I got my bachelor's degree in chemistry."

"Did you?" Josh looked impressed. "You're full of surprises, aren't you?"

Angie gave a little shrug. "You don't really have to know that much about chemistry to be a good baker."

"You are a woman of many talents, it seems."

Angie and Josh continued their bantering while they sipped their wine. After a half hour, Angie knew she had to get going so that there would be time to do her errand, make dinner, and work on Jenna's jewelry.

Josh said, "We're having an open house at the resort next weekend to celebrate the renovations. It's going to be appetizers and desserts, open bar. We're having local people provide the food and flowers. We're paying them of course. Betty Hayes is supplying the flowers from her green house and the local floral designer is going to make arrangements with them. We're getting in touch with local caterers. I was going to ask you if you'd like to do the desserts."

Angie wondered if Josh had wanted to have a drink together in order to get her to do the desserts at a reduced cost. Her heart sank.

"But...." Josh said.

"But, what?" Angie asked.

"I'd rather have you there as a guest. So you could enjoy yourself. Would you like to come? Your sisters, too? We're inviting the townspeople to come by and join us from 7-10pm. Since you've never been to the resort, you might enjoy seeing it." Josh added, "Of course, if you'd like the contract to do the desserts, it's yours."

Flickers of attraction to Josh tickled Angie's skin. It's probably dumb to start something with him. That's if he feels the same way I do, which maybe he doesn't and I'm concocting the whole idea. He and his brother will just move out of the area as soon as their latest projects are all set.

Angie ignored the thoughts running through her head. "We're going to be really busy over the next couple of weeks."

The smile dropped from Josh's face, assuming

Angie was going to refuse the invitation to the reception.

"So I don't think it would be wise to take on the contract to do the desserts. But it might be nice to come. I'll talk to my sisters. A night out would do all of us good."

Josh beamed at her from across the table.

15

It was a warm, sunny, late afternoon when Tom's truck pulled into the Victorian's driveway and Angie and Jenna came out to meet him. After several delays and numerous rescheduling, Tom was finally able to come to the house to look over what the girls wanted for renovations in order to suit the new businesses they planned to run out of the house.

"Morning." Tom called out to the girls as they came down the porch steps with Euclid trailing behind them. Euclid was a house cat for the most part, but occasionally he went in the yard with Angie or one of her sisters. He enjoyed sitting in the sunshine and he always stayed close by and never strayed beyond the property line of the Victorian.

Euclid rubbed himself against Tom's legs and purred. "Hello, buddy." Tom scratched Euclid's cheeks and chest.

"Someone has a friend." Jenna had her long hair up in a high ponytail and was wearing a navy blue tank top and white shorts. She flashed Tom a brilliant smile. Angie eyed her sister and wondered how she'd missed the obvious attraction Jenna had for Tom.

"I've done some small repairs for Professor Linden," Tom said. "Euclid and I are old friends."

They walked to the side of the house where there was another set of steps that led to the wraparound porch. "This is where I'd like the entrance to the bake shop to be." Angie pointed to the wall where there was a window in place. If I use this room for the main part of the café then people could enter through the new door. The room right here has access to the kitchen."

"Let's go in so I can take a look." Tom started up the steps of the porch.

"Come in this way," Jenna said. "I can show you the room where I've set up my jewelry workshop."

They walked along the porch and Jenna opened a French door that led to her workshop.

"This looks great." Tom admired the space. "The professor called this the music room."

Jenna nodded. "My customers will be able to come up the porch steps and come right into the jewelry shop. We're going to bring in two antique glass fronted cabinets to use as display cases for finished designs." Jenna indicated where they would place the cases.

"Perfect," Tom said. "So you'll be ready to open to customers soon. No renovations needed in here."

"Yeah. I'll still run my online shop, too. This will just be for summer customers who stop in. Right now, I'm behind on my online orders. I'll get this set up as soon as I can."

"Glad to help with any heavy moving that needs to be done." Tom smiled at Jenna.

Angie wanted to tease them for the bit of flirtation that was going back and forth, but she decided to hold her tongue for a while and pretend she didn't notice. She was entertained by the energy that was buzzing between Jenna and Tom and she couldn't wait until later when she could really razz her sister for the crush she had on him.

They moved from Jenna's workshop to a hallway that led to the large room that Angie wanted to use as the customer part of the bake shop. The space had big windows that let in the natural light and looked out onto the porch.

"So here's the room I thought would be perfect," Angie said. "If we changed that window to a door, it could be the entrance to the café. And over here," she pointed, "the kitchen is on the other side of this wall. If you made a door here, I can get in to do the baking."

Tom had his measuring tape out and a small notebook where he was jotting the information down. Euclid had perched on a chair next to the window to watch what Tom was doing.

"I think Euclid is going to help you with the renovations." Angie patted the cat behind the ears.

"When I've worked in the house before, Euclid was my right-hand man." Tom made some more notes. "This looks good, Angie. You can put the counters here. You can use this section for the coffee bar, put the customer stools over here." He winked at the girls. "I want to be sure my usual seat is accounted for."

Jenna and Angie laughed. "Don't worry," Jenna said. "Angie already planned where your own personal stool will go."

"That was the first thing I considered," Angie joked.

"Glad you didn't forget me." Tom took another measurement. "Let's go see the kitchen. If you're planning on running a bed and breakfast and a café out of here, there are certain kitchen requirements that have to be met."

As they headed to the kitchen, Angie looked worried. "I forgot about that. I'd better go to the town hall right away to get approval to run the businesses out of the house."

"You'll need that in hand before I can apply for the renovation permits," Tom told her. "You shouldn't have any trouble getting the okay from the town."

In the kitchen Tom made some suggestions that weren't very elaborate in order to keep costs under control, but that would make the work flow more smoothly once the businesses got underway. Angie liked his ideas and hoped that the work estimate would be within her budget.

"There's just one more thing I'd like you to put in your estimate. We'd like to put a door at the top of the third floor stairs. We're planning to use that floor as our private space and we want to have a door with a lock to keep the B and B clients from wandering up there."

"Before we go upstairs to show you where we'd

like the door installed," Jenna said, "how about some iced tea? It's warm today. We can sit out on the porch." She flashed Tom a warm smile. "Do you have time?"

Tom checked his watch. "I have another project to give an estimate on, but a cold drink sounds good."

Angie took glasses down from the cabinet and Jenna removed a glass pitcher of iced tea from the refrigerator. She put the glasses on a tray while Angie placed some chocolate chip scones on a plate. They took everything out to the porch and sat in rocking chairs to enjoy the refreshments.

"How are you girls holding up working day and night between the two businesses?" Tom sipped his iced tea.

"We don't sleep much." Angie laughed.

"We couldn't keep it up forever, that's for sure, but we're doing okay." Jenna bit into a scone. "Angie's treats keep us going." She grinned.

"Ellie's here now. She's been getting things ready to open the bed and breakfast," Angie said. "She helps out with the jewelry making in the evenings. We try to make it a fun thing. We light a fire, play music, and make sure there are plenty of things to eat."

"Doesn't sound half bad." Tom reached for another scone. "Delicious as usual, Angie."

"Where's Euclid? Jenna looked around the porch for the cat.

"He stayed inside," Angie said. "He was curled up on top of the fridge."

"I'm surprised he stayed in. He's usually in the middle of things when we're doing anything. He doesn't miss a trick that one." Jenna brushed some crumbs off of her tank top.

"It seems strange with the professor gone." Tom looked off across the front lawn. "She always had something or other for me to do, small things. Most contractors wouldn't have bothered with her business, they'd send her to a handyman, but I liked her. I liked helping her out, talking with her. She was an interesting person, a good lady."

"I miss her coming into the shop everyday," Angie said.

"Poisoned." Tom shook his head. "It's hard to believe."

"Why would someone poison her?" Jenna's face was sad.

"I guess more important," Tom said, "is who poisoned her?"

"I just can't stand thinking a murderer is on the

loose in Sweet Cove." A shiver ran down Jenna's back.

"Did you notice anything that day?" Angie turned towards Tom. "I keep going over it, and going over it, but I just can't think of anything out of the ordinary." She sighed. "I didn't notice anyone near the professor's drink. But I wasn't watching it closely either. "

"I was on my usual stool," Tom said. "I had my back to the professor. I didn't see anything. Things seemed normal in there that day."

Euclid meowed from the other side of the open window.

"I'll let him out." Jenna got up and opened the front door so Euclid could join them on the porch.

The cat pranced out the door as soon as it opened. As Jenna watched him pass her, she noticed something. "Euclid has something in his mouth."

"Oh, no." Angie cringed. "I hope it isn't a mouse."

"He's bringing you a present." Tom chuckled.

Euclid approached Angie's rocking chair and laid something at her feet.

"What's this?" Angie reached down to pick up Euclid's gift. Her eyes went wide when she saw what it was.

"What is it?" Jenna looked over at Angie as she returned to her rocking chair.

Angie held her hand out so they could see what she was holding.

"A piece of cloth?" Jenna leaned closer.

Angie's heart pounded and a shiver shook her stomach.

"A bow tie?" Tom reached for it.

Angie's face hardened. "It's a bow tie all right." Her voice trembled.

Jenna asked, "Where'd that come from?"

"Jack Ford wears bow ties." Angie's breath was fast and shallow as she eyed the tie. Anger flooded her body.

"Did it fall off of him the day of the remembrance reception?" Jenna asked

"No. He had on a bright yellow and blue bow tie that day. It stood out to me." Angie took a deep breath and when she spoke, her voice was hard. "He must have lost this one in his haste to get out of the house. The night he broke in here."

"What?" Tom nearly jumped from the rocker. "He broke into your house?"

"We've been speculating." Jenna got up and reached for the bow tie in Tom's hand. She looked it over. "You know we told you that someone was upstairs the night Angie came here to feed Euclid after the professor died?"

"Yeah," Tom said, "but you never mentioned you thought it might be the lawyer. I know he is an odd duck, but to break into a house?"

Angie told Tom what she overheard when she was at Jack Ford's law office. "He said something like 'I couldn't get it with her in the house.'"

"What was he talking about?" Tom bristled with anger and shot off more questions. "What was he after? What was missing from the house?"

"I don't know what he was talking about," Angie said. "I have no idea what he was looking for."

"We don't know if anything is missing because we don't know what the professor had in the house," Jenna explained. "But if what Angie heard is an indication, then he didn't find what he was looking for."

"Tell the police." Tom scowled.

"We have no proof of anything. We can't even prove the bow tie belongs to Jack Ford," Angie said. "So there's no use telling the police anything."

Euclid was sitting on top of the porch railing watching Angie. He let out an angry meow and Angie startled. "Euclid, jeez."

Jenna, Tom, and Angie rocked in their chairs for

a few minutes and thought about what had been going on.

Angie said, "I have an idea." She took the bow tie from Jenna. "I have an appointment next week with Attorney Ford to sign the will he drew up for me." Angie made eye contact with Euclid and gripped the bow tie tight in her hand. "I'm sure Mr. Ford will be very happy when I return his bow tie to him."

16

Angie, Jenna, Ellie, and Courtney stepped out of the car and headed for the front entrance of the resort. The hotel-restaurant had lush landscaping and there were pots of pansies and tulips placed along the walkways. Hidden lighting under the bushes and trees illuminated the leaves and bark and there was a water feature in front of the portico area with a circular driveway leading to the front door.

"Why haven't we come here before?" Courtney wore her long, honey blonde hair loose and cascading down her back. Her legs looked even longer because of the heels she was wearing. "This place is swanky."

"We haven't been here before because we can't

afford it," Jenna said. She had on a coral spring dress and gold sandals.

Angie smoothed her hair. Her black skirt hugged her curves, and her necklace of black and silver stones accented her crisp white blouse. The necklace was one of Jenna's designs and had been a birthday gift to Angie.

Ellie walked behind them looking out over the darkening ocean and glancing across the lawns to where their grandmother's cottage used to be. Angie looked back to her sister and when Ellie approached, she slipped her arm around her sister's waist.

"I haven't been down here on the point for a long time." Ellie ran her hand over her long, pale blonde hair and pulled it forward over her shoulder. "It's funny, isn't it? How things change?"

Since parking the car, Angie had felt a subtle humming sensation running through her veins. It wasn't unpleasant or bothersome. It was more like a heightened awareness of everything around her. It happened every time she was on the point. "Do you feel different when you're here?"

"What do you mean?" Ellie asked.

"I don't know, sort of aware of things."

"No different than usual. Just sad, remembering Nana."

Angie nodded. It wasn't just sadness, it was something else, but she couldn't figure out the words to describe how she felt.

They entered the lobby. Many of the people milling about paused for a second in their conversations as the young women walked in together.

Angie expected the lobby to be decorated in shades of green and blue to evoke the seaside location, and she was surprised to see the muted shades of plum, mocha, and cream on the furniture, rugs, and wall colors. The area was softly lit and candles were placed in large glass containers scattered about the space projecting a sense of calm and luxury.

"This is beautiful," Courtney said.

Angie could see that Ellie was taking it all in, probably imagining what she could do to the Victorian's bed and breakfast areas that would evoke similar feelings of relaxation and comfort in her guests.

The girls followed the crowd through the lobby and into the restaurant. The space was huge, but the arrangement of the furniture and the way it was lit made the room feel elegant and comfortable. The far side of the room had a curved wall with floor to ceiling windows overlooking the ocean. Candles and cut glass chandeliers cast a soft glow over the guests. Buffet tables decorated with flowers and fresh fruit arrangements held hot and cold appetizers, and several kinds of pastries and desserts. Tucked to one side there was an open bar with several bartenders serving drinks to the guests. A jazz band played in the corner close to the windows.

"Wow." Courtney's blue eyes widened taking in the beauty of the room. She looked at Angie. "I'm so glad you agreed to come to this thing tonight."

"Angie." A voice called out to her. She turned to see Josh Williams crossing the room towards her. He looked handsome in a fitted dark blue suit. "I'm so glad you came. You all look beautiful."

Angie introduced Josh to Ellie and Courtney. Josh said hello to Jenna. The five of them talked for a few minutes and then Jenna, pretending she was hungry but really wanting to give Angie time with Josh, herded her sisters over to the food tables.

"Everything is lovely," Angie said. "I don't know what it was like before, but it's gorgeous now."

Josh smiled. He looked pleased and proud. "It makes me happy that you like it."

"It's a great turnout." Angie looked around at all

the people standing or sitting in groups enjoying themselves.

Josh nodded. "Would you like something to eat? The desserts are good but not nearly up to your standards." He grinned. "I tried to get the best baker in town to make the desserts for tonight, but she was too busy."

"That's really too bad." Angie's eyes twinkled. "Maybe she can help you out another time."

"I certainly hope so." The way Josh looked at her made Angie's heart skip a beat.

"Josh." Davis Williams came up behind them. He nodded at Angie. "Hello." Davis turned to his brother. "I've been looking for you. Adam Prescott wants to speak with us. He has some land up in Newburyport that he wants developed."

"Can't you take a rest from business and just enjoy the evening?" Josh gave his brother a serious look.

"Prescott's waiting for us." Davis started to steer his brother away.

Josh gave Angie a look like he was being dragged to the gallows. "I'll be back."

Angie gave him a little wave goodbye. She looked around the room for her sisters and saw Lisa

Barrows standing by the entryway holding a clipboard.

"Lisa." Angie came up beside her.

"Angie. Hi. How are you?" Lisa's face looked pale and there were slight dark circles under her eyes like she hadn't been sleeping. "I didn't expect you to be here."

Angie thought that when she ran into Lisa again, she would appear her old self, but her former employee looked worn out and harried. Angie could feel a negative energy from Lisa, an anxiousness that seemed to ooze from her pores. She wondered if Lisa was seeing a doctor.

"Why, not? The whole town was invited. We had to take advantage of free food." Angie joked, but it fell flat with Lisa. "How are you doing? How is your new job going?"

"It's okay. It's always busy here. I work all the time. It's sort of demanding." She glanced at her clipboard.

Angie said, "Sounds a lot like the bake shop. You always handled that well so you must be doing great here."

Lisa shrugged. "Is everything going okay for you?" she managed to ask.

"Yeah, everything's good. The girls are all here. I'll tell them to come by and say hello."

Lisa nodded. "Okay. I have to go check on the kitchen. I'll see you later." She forced a tiny smile and exited the room in a hurry.

When Angie found her sisters, they were sitting at a table near the windows eating. She told them she'd run into Lisa and how she seemed exhausted and nervous.

"She must be working hard trying to do a really good job since she's new here," Ellie said.

Jenna said to Angie, "I bet she feels uncomfortable around you for quitting like she did."

"She probably does." Angie looked over at the food spread over the buffet tables. "I'm starving." She got up, headed to the buffet, loaded a plate with food, and returned to sit. She lifted her fork to her mouth.

"Do you think the professor's killer is here?" Ellie asked.

A chill rippled down Angie's back and she stared across the room. Her internal humming sensation seemed to have ratcheted up a notch.

"Angie?"

"Huh? What?" She blinked at Ellie.

"Are you spacing out?"

"I guess I did." She took a sip from her glass of water.

"There's Police Chief Martin over there." Jenna turned to Angie. "Did he ever tell you what kind of poison was used to kill Professor Linden?"

"No." Angie put her fork down. She seemed to have lost her appetite. "He said he wasn't able to say since it's an ongoing investigation."

Courtney said, "It could have been anything. There are lots of poisonous things that anyone could get their hands on."

"Like what?" Ellie's forehead creased with worry.

"Well..." Courtney said. "Look at the centerpiece. There's oleander and lily of the valley in it. Those plants are poisonous. Grind them up and put them in tea or coffee, and...."

"Really?" Ellie leaned back, horrified.

Angie looked at the seemingly innocent flowers in the center of the table, and then the color drained out of her face. She inhaled a quick breath.

Jenna turned to her. "What's wrong with you?"

Angie swallowed. "The flowers in the center-pieces, they came from Betty Hayes' greenhouse."

"So?" Jenna's face was puzzled.

"Betty Hayes pressed Professor Linden to sell the Victorian. The agent's commission would be huge on a sale like that. The professor considered selling her house not long ago, but she changed her mind."

Jenna lowered her voice. "Did Betty...?"

Ellie's fingers trembled as she touched her temple. "Did Betty kill the professor?"

"So she could get the commission." Courtney leaned close. "Betty knew the professor had no relatives. Betty's the only Realtor in town. The lawyer would have given her the listing."

"There she is over there." The three sisters followed Jenna's gaze across the room where Betty was talking animatedly to Josh and Davis and Adam Prescott. "They better watch out for her."

"How much of a plant would you need to kill someone?" Angie asked Courtney.

"Not much. Just grind some up. Steep it in boiling water. Then add some of the water to whatever someone is drinking."

"How do you know this stuff?" Angie's face was pale.

Courtney made a face. "I watch crime shows."

Jenna said, "The professor had a heart condition."

Courtney glanced around to make sure no one was standing nearby. "With a heart condition, it wouldn't take much to kill her. Her heart would go into A-Fib. She might even have a seizure."

"That's exactly what happened." Angie's eyes filled with tears remembering the professor on the ground next to her front porch stairs. "This is awful. I was just at Betty's house the other day."

"We need to tell the chief what we think about Betty," Courtney said.

"Not here, though. Not tonight." Angie brushed at her eyes. "We could be wrong about her. It could be someone else that did it."

"It's possible. But we should tell the chief anyway. He comes into the shop in the afternoons sometimes," Jenna said. "There aren't as many people in the shop at that time. We can tell him then."

17

A ngie arrived for her appointment at Attorney Jack Ford's office a few minutes early. She introduced herself to the receptionist and took a seat pretending to look through a magazine, but in reality she was too on edge to focus on any of the articles. Angie tried to distract herself by thinking about the Victorian's renovations, but her thoughts kept jumping to Jack Ford, his bow tie, and why he had been in her house.

Angie had to admit that it wasn't her house when Ford broke into the mansion, and technically it wasn't her house now either since she had to wait for the probate proceedings to be completed before the deed was in her possession. The professor owned the house and was dead. The professor had no relatives and the recipients of the inheritance didn't own anything yet, so who was in charge of the house? Jack Ford. He was the professor's administrator and he had a key to the Victorian. It couldn't be said that he broke in then, since he had a key as well as the authority to check on the house. Why didn't I think of this before? But why did he run when he heard me in the house? And why was the house dark? What was he up to that he needed to run away from the premises?

"Ms. Roseland." The receptionist stood a few feet from Angie.

Angie looked up. It was clear that the receptionist had called her name more than once. Flustered, Angie picked up her purse and jacket and followed the woman into Ford's office.

Ford was behind his desk when Angie entered, and he stood to greet her. He wore a brown, tweed jacket, crisp white shirt, and a yellow bow tie. He was about Angie's height and he had a lean build. Angie thought that if he wasn't so twitchy and severe that he could be considered quite good-looking.

Ford's movements were quick and efficient as he extended his arm over the desk to give Angie's hand a hurried shake. "Please, sit. I hope you're doing well."

Angie took a seat in one of the chairs in front of the dark, wooden desk. "Yes, thank you."

"Everything is in order with the will and is ready for your signature." Ford removed the paperwork from a leather folder and placed it on the desk in front of Angie so that she could examine it. "Please read it over to be sure it is satisfactory."

Angie took a few minutes to review the will. "It all looks fine to me."

"Very good." Ford buzzed his receptionist to come in. "Mrs. Adams will act as signatory witness."

Ford placed a silver pen in front of Angie and gave one to Mrs. Adams. He opened the documents to the correct pages and indicated where each should sign. Ford signed both copies and nodded to Mrs. Adams that she was dismissed. "I will keep one copy here on file in the office." He folded the second copy, inserted it into an envelope, and handed it to Angie. "This is an original of the will as you requested."

"Thank you." Angie placed the envelope in her purse.

"How are things at the Victorian?" Ford asked. "Any issues that I should be aware of?"

"Nothing. No problems have come up. I had a contractor take a look at the house and he'll be sending me an estimate for the renovations I'd like to have done." Angie gave Ford a pointed look. "I understand that nothing can be started until I have the deed to the home."

Ford nodded. He had remained straight-faced and without expression throughout the interaction with Angie. She wondered if he was always so formal and humorless. She had yet to see even a glimmer of a smile on his face. Everything was businesslike and direct, no chit chat at all, only the most minor polite questions.

"Is there anything else I can do for you?" Ford was ready to send Angie on her way.

Angie's heart started to pound. "Oh, I nearly forgot," she lied. She reached into her purse and removed the bow tie. She placed it on Ford's desk.

"I think you left this behind when you were in the Victorian." Angie watched the lawyer's face closely.

Ford regarded the tie. Something flickered over his face and was gone, his usual blank expression remaining intact. "I don't believe I'm missing a tie."

Angie narrowed her eyes at Ford. "I don't know anyone else in Sweet Cove who wears a bow tie."

"Well." He shook his head. "I don't recognize it."

"You must have a large collection, then." Angie

leaned against the chair back and folded her hands in her lap to indicate that she wasn't quite ready to leave the office. She waited to see if Ford would say anything more.

Ford shifted in his seat about to stand up when Angie said, "Attorney Ford, I think we need to have a talk." She glanced at the open office door. "A private talk."

Angie thought she noticed a pink tinge on Ford's cheeks as he rose, walked over to the door, closed it, and returned to his desk chair.

"What would you like to discuss, Ms. Roseland?"

Angie used a courteous tone when she said, "Why were you in the Victorian on the night that Professor Linden died?"

Ford cleared his throat. "The night the professor died?"

Angie exhaled loudly. "I know you have a key to the house. I know you're the administrator of the estate and you have the right to inspect the property." Angie paused. "So I wonder why you ran from the house when I showed up to take care of the cat."

"I didn't run from the house." Ford seemed to think that anyone who ran anywhere would be considered most undignified. "You were in the house that night? I didn't know that. If I recall correctly, I believe I stopped by the Victorian to look for some paperwork, to be sure I was in possession of Professor Linden's most recent will."

"You left the back door unlocked," Angie told him.

"Did I?"

Angie had to keep from rolling her eyes. He's good, coming up with a story on the fly like this. "When I was here previously to discuss the preparation of my will, I arrived early. I overheard you speaking on the phone. You said something like, 'I couldn't spend time looking for it with her downstairs in the house' and 'I'll take care of it.' Is there something you want from the Victorian?"

The tiniest smile played over the attorney's mouth and for a moment, Angie thought he was going to be straight with her, but then he batted the air with his hand. "Ms. Roseland, you can't imagine that everything is about you and the Victorian. I have many clients. I'm not sure what you overheard, but there is nothing sinister at work. I assure you, I have only your best interests in mind."

As annoyance and exhaustion flooded Angie's body, she felt reprimanded by the attorney and for a second wondered if everything he was saying was true. Then, why do I always feel like he's about to tell me something more and then changes his mind at the last second? Ford had an answer for everything. She felt like she would never get anything important out of him.

Just as she was about to get up to leave, Angie remembered something else. She knew Ford would dismiss what she was about to ask, but Angie wanted him to know that she was aware that the professor had met with him about this. "Shortly before Professor Linden's passing, I understand that she came to see you. She wanted to know something about her father."

Ford let out a long breath. "Client confidentiality prevents me from discussing client meetings or the content of such meetings."

Angie had to use all of her will power not to fling herself over the desk and strangle Ford. She nodded and stood up. "Have a pleasant afternoon, Attorney Ford."

"And you, Ms. Roseland. I'll be in touch as probate proceeds on the estate." He almost smiled.

Angie turned and left the office. When she reached the sidewalk, she swallowed her anger and frustration and bit the inside of her cheek to keep from bursting into tears.

ANGIE WALKED to her bake shop covering the distance in record time. She was full of negative energy and even though all of tomorrow's bakery treats had been prepared and were ready to go, she needed to be moving around and working with her hands. She threw her jacket on the back of one of the café chairs and pulled a fresh apron over her head and tied it in back. She flicked the lights on in the back room and hurried about pulling out flour, sugar, butter, salt, and milk. Angie decided to make a few fruit pies. She'd bring one home for dessert tonight and put the other two out for the customers tomorrow.

Bustling around the room helped her pent up emotions start to wind down. Just as she was measuring out the flour, she heard a knock on the café door. Angie sighed. Someone must have seen the light and thought we were open. She wiped her hands on a cloth, and hurried to the front of the shop to inform the person that the shop was closed. Jenna's face was peering through the glass window of the door.

Angie hurried to unlock it. Jenna swept inside.

Tom stood in the doorway. "So how did it go? Did you whoop that lawyer into shape?"

Before she could say a word, Angie burst into tears. Tom's eyes widened in surprise and he wrapped Angie in a bear hug. She buried her face into the front of Tom's flannel work shirt. Still holding her, Tom moved Angie into the shop and Jenna shut the door. "What on earth happened?"

Embarrassed, Angie stepped away from Tom and pulled the hem of her apron up to wipe the tears from her face. She sat down at one of the café tables. Tom sat too and Jenna hurried to get a glass of water for her sister. Angie sipped the cool water and held the glass against her temple.

"I'm sorry. I'm an idiot."

Jenna put her hand over Angie's. "Tell us."

Angie explained everything that had gone on at Attorney Ford's office. "He probably didn't do anything wrong at all. He was probably just doing what he says, looking for a copy of the professor's will. He's the administrator of the estate. He can go into the house. And of course he can't divulge anything that he and the professor talked about in private. I don't even know why I brought it up." She stared at her glass and groaned. "I felt like a little kid being scolded by some old man."

"Yes. Old. He's probably Tom's age," Jenna said, with a sly smile.

Tom scowled. "I'm just a few years older than you."

"Ancient," Jenna teased.

Tom ignored the comment. "The way Ford dresses and his body language makes him seem like he's an old man. Don't pay any attention to him, Angie. I still think he was up to no good, skulking around in your house. Why didn't he just say hello when he heard you in the house that night? Why were the lights off? Running away makes him look suspicious."

"I agree." Jenna nodded. "I think we still need to be careful of him."

Angie let out a sigh. "You're right. Why were the lights off?" Just sitting and talking with Tom and Jenna helped to dissipate her tension. They were right. They needed to be on guard around Ford.

She had to remember to ask Police Chief Martin if he had given a new key to Attorney Ford when he arranged to have the locks changed at the house. Angie didn't want Ford being able to enter the Victorian whenever he pleased. She didn't think it would be wrong to limit his access to the house to only pre-arranged times.

Angie looked at Tom and Jenna and narrowed her eyes. "Why are you two together anyway?" To Angie's knowledge, the two of them had never spent any time alone with one another.

A blush tinged Jenna's cheeks and she started stammering.

Tom said, "We just ran into each other here in town."

"Oh?" The corners of Angie's mouth turned up and she looked at them suspiciously. "You just ran into each other? Your meeting wasn't planned?"

"What? No." Jenna pushed a strand of her soft, brown hair away from her face. In order to avoid Angie's scrutiny, she got up and went to the counter to make herself a latte.

"Hmm." Angie turned to Tom without saying a word. She formed a heart with the fingers of her hands and held it in front of her chest. She had to suppress a chuckle when Tom rolled his eyes at her.

18

Angie was refilling Tom's coffee when Josh Williams entered the bake shop and when he saw Angie standing behind the counter, his face lit up. While smiling at Angie, he greeted Tom and sat down on the counter stool next to him. Josh's smile sent tingles skittering over Angie's skin and she was almost embarrassed at the effect Josh had on her.

"Coffee?" Angie's eyes sparkled.

Tom caught the look on Angie's face and his eyebrows went up.

"Yes, please. I'll be right back." Josh headed to the men's room.

"What's this?" Tom questioned.

Angie turned to reach for a clean mug. "What's

what?" When she faced the counter and put the mug down at Josh's place, she saw a sly grin on Tom's face.

"What's going here?" Tom's question was tinged with a teasing tone.

"Where?" Angie tried to avoid Tom's interrogation. She filled Josh's mug with coffee.

"Well, when Josh came in something like flirting seemed to fill the air between you."

Angie scowled. "Hush, you. Here he comes."

Josh sat down and sipped his coffee.

"So, Josh, anything new?" Tom looked like he was about to chuckle. Angie narrowed her eyes at him.

"The reception really went well the other night. Did you enjoy yourselves?" Josh directed the question more at Angie than Tom.

"It was great. We had a very nice time," Angie told him. As she moved away to wait on other customers, she shot Tom a warning look. Tom smiled at her innocently.

Angie kept glancing over at Tom wondering what he was talking to Josh about and hoping he wasn't going to embarrass her. Her heart pounded double time. When she was packaging some donuts into a box for a customer, Tom got up from his stool, and called, "See you tomorrow, Angie." Angie looked over at him, standing slightly behind Josh. Tom formed the shape of a heart with his fingers and held them next to his chest.

The scowl she shot Tom quickly turned to a smile when she caught Josh looking at her.

"More coffee?" Angie asked sweetly.

"Please. Tom's a nice guy. We were talking about him doing some work for us on some projects we might have planned."

Angie wanted to groan imagining Tom having plenty of opportunity to tease her and Josh if anything happened between them. "Tom's a great guy. I've seen his work. It's excellent. He's a careful craftsman. Very knowledgeable."

"I'm sorry I didn't have much time to talk to you at the resort open house the other night."

"That's okay. We had a really nice time. My sisters and I haven't been out together like that for such a long time. It was fun."

"It was a huge turnout. We were pleased that so many people from town showed up."

"I ran into my former employee, Lisa Barrows. She said the resort was keeping her busy."

"Lisa gave her notice the other day," Josh said. "Did she tell you?"

Angie's eyes widened and her jaw dropped. "No,

she didn't tell me. She's quitting? She's only been there a week."

"She's moving back to central Massachusetts. She said it's all been too much change for her too fast." Josh lifted the mug and sipped his coffee.

Angie said, "Her mom passed away a year ago. Professor Linden's death hit her hard. She seems really stressed lately." Angie felt badly for Lisa. Lisa wanted to make her retirement home in Sweet Cove and Angie was sorry that things didn't work out the way Lisa had planned.

"Well, I hope things will be better for her when she makes the move," Josh said. "She doesn't seem happy at all."

"Maybe I'll invite her to dinner before she leaves." Something about what she was hearing about Lisa made Angie uneasy. Something flickered in her mind, but then was gone.

Josh's phone buzzed and he checked it. "Davis is after me." He grinned and reached for his mug. "It's all work with him, no down time." Josh took the last swallow of his coffee. He seemed like he wanted to say something. He hesitated, but then blurted, "I was wondering if you'd like to go for a bike ride on the Sunday after you close up the shop. I thought you might be at a loss for what to do without having to be at the bake shop that day. It might be a nice distraction."

Angie's heart fluttered at Josh's thoughtfulness. "I'd like that."

Josh beamed at her. It seemed like his whole body flooded with energy at Angie's positive answer. "I'll come by the Victorian about 2pm?"

Little flashes of electricity bounced between them.

"I'll be ready."

THE GIRLS SET up a long wooden table in the music room of the Victorian. It was covered with beading tools, silver findings, and containers of beads made of silver, gold, pearl, shell, and glass, in every color imaginable. The music room had large windows overlooking the back yard and a door led to the wraparound porch. The sisters thought the room turned out to be a perfect jewelry shop for Jenna's business. One wall had built-in wood cabinets and shelves where Jenna could store her pieces. In a few days, they planned to bring in the two antique cases that would display the finished jewelry. Jenna could work at a table by the windows while customers browsed the cases.

Ellie had moved into the Victorian a few days ago after finishing her work at the Boston hotel. She was spending the days building a website for the new bed and breakfast, applying for permits, cleaning, organizing, and ordering some new linens for the bedrooms. Ellie was researching the most cost effective way to advertise the B and B since they had a very small budget.

Jenna, Angie, and Ellie perched at the work table putting the pieces together following Jenna's designs. There were a lot of online orders to finish and send out. It was a cool early May evening, and the girls had made a fire in the room's ornately carved fireplace. Euclid slept, curled up on the rug in front of the crackling fire.

"So Lisa quit and is moving away?" Jenna used a tool to crimp a small silver bead in place. "The professor's death must have really taken a toll on her."

Euclid lifted his head.

Ellie picked up a silver clasp to attach to the bracelet she had just strung together. "You said her mom passed away not long ago. Maybe it's all just too upsetting for her. It was probably too soon to move to another place."

A flare of anxiety pulsed through Angie's veins. She put down the necklace she had been working on and watched the flames dancing in the fireplace. Euclid sat up and stared at her. When Angie shifted her gaze and met Euclid's eyes, she opened her mouth in surprise at the thought that flashed in her mind. She dropped the tool she was holding and her sisters looked up.

"What's wrong?" Jenna asked.

"I just had an idea." Angie's hands trembled. "What if Lisa saw something the day the professor died."

Ellie and Jenna had puzzled looks on their faces.

"What if she saw someone put something in the professor's drink? Maybe she's afraid to come forward and tell. Maybe she's afraid the killer will come after her." Angie's heart was racing.

"That's why she's been so upset." Ellie's eyes were wide.

"It makes sense." Excitement flowed through Jenna's voice. "That's why she quit the bake shop. She must have seen the person there almost every day."

"That poor woman, she must be afraid for her

life." Angie stood up and started to pace around the room.

Euclid let out a low hiss.

"She knows who did it," Angie said. "But she's afraid to tell. I bet she suspects someone but is afraid to speak up. Or...what if the killer threatened her?"

A low guttural growl vibrated in Euclid's throat.

"I need to talk to her." Angie stopped pacing and stared at her sisters. "I'll invite her to dinner. I'll go to the resort and ask her in person. It will be harder to refuse me if I ask her in person."

"How will you get Lisa to admit what she saw? Who, she saw?" Jenna twirled a bead between her fingers as she thought.

Ellie straightened. "Tell her you think you saw something. Tell her you think you saw someone put something in the professor's drink, but you aren't sure, and you don't want to name the person unless somebody else has suspicion. Ask her if she saw anything that day. Maybe when you tell her you're suspicious of someone, she'll feel safe telling you what she saw."

Angie's face lit up. "You're a genius." She hugged Ellie. "Now I just have to get her to talk to me. I'll go to the resort after work tomorrow and invite her to go to dinner."

19

F or the second time in a few days, Angie parked her car in the lot of the resort. Her cell phone beeped with an incoming text just as she turned the car off. It was from Jenna telling her to call as soon as she was done talking to Lisa. Jenna and Ellie were driving up the coast to a nearby mall to search for some new window treatments for a few of the bedrooms they'd be using for the B and B.

Sitting in the driver's seat, Angie reached for the door handle and the quick movement of her head caused a wave of dizziness to engulf her. She leaned her head against the headrest and took in some deep breaths. What was that about? She gingerly opened the car door and stepped out. Feeling steady, she headed for the entrance of the resort. The closer she got to the door, the more she felt the strange thrumming beating in her blood. Is there some weird magnetic field around here that makes me feel this every time I'm on the point? She tried to ignore the sensation by focusing her attention on how pretty the area looked in the glow of the setting sun.

Angie walked through the lobby and approached the registration area where she asked the desk clerk if he could call Lisa Barrows to the lobby for a moment. He agreed, and Angie moved to a group of sofas set up in the middle of the lobby.

A few minutes later, Lisa came around the corner and when she spotted Angie, she stopped short. Trying to recover from the surprise of seeing her former employer waiting for her, Lisa plastered a smile on her face. "Oh, Angie. Hello. This is a surprise."

"Hi. How are you?" Angie moved closer to Lisa. "I ran into Josh Williams and he said you were moving back to central Massachusetts."

Lisa nodded. She looked down at the floor. Angie thought Lisa might elaborate on the reasons for her sudden decision to leave Sweet Cove or at least say something about how she thought it would be a good move for her, but she remained silent.

"I came to ask you to join me for dinner," Angie said cheerfully. "I'd like to take you out for a nice meal to thank you for all the hours you put in at the bake shop."

Lisa's face flushed and she started to stammer, "I ... I'm working...."

Josh came out of the restaurant just then and saw Angie and Lisa talking together. He smiled brightly at Angie as he walked over to the women. "Hey."

Angie greeted Josh with a warm smile. He was such a welcome contrast to Lisa's nervous and withdrawn manner. "I came to ask Lisa to dinner. Since she's moving away, I'd like to take her to dinner as a thank you for working at my shop and to wish her well."

"That's great. What a terrific idea."

"I don't get off for two more hours though," Lisa said.

Josh turned to Lisa. "Oh. Go ahead with Angie. It's quiet here now. I'll pay you for your full shift. No worries. Go ahead and have a nice meal together."

Angie was impressed by Josh's kindness. He made her feel warm and happy.

"I don't think I should do that," Lisa started to object, but Josh cut her off.

"I insist. You've been working hard. Take the time

for a nice meal. In fact," Josh looked towards the resort restaurant. "Please have dinner here. It's my treat to both of you."

"How generous," Angie smiled. "Thank you." She didn't think she would have been able to convince Lisa to eat with her, but now that Josh made the offer to have dinner at the resort, it would be very awkward for Lisa to refuse. Angie wanted to kiss Josh, and not just because his suggestion made it easier for her to get Lisa to join her.

Lisa gave off the nervous vibe of a trapped animal. Her lips turned down and her shoulders drooped. Angie put her hand on Lisa's arm and gently nudged her towards the restaurant. "This will be perfect."

Josh walked with them and spoke to the restaurant hostess, and then he turned to leave. "Enjoy dinner," he told Angie and Lisa.

The hostess led the women to a small table by the windows. She handed them menus.

"It's beautiful here." Angie opened her menu and looked over the choices. "I bet you're looking forward to getting back to your old town and relaxing for a while."

Lisa sipped from her water glass. "Yeah. I think it's for the best. I made too many changes too soon."

"It was a big adjustment when I moved up here from Boston last year to open the shop," Angie said. "Even though I was familiar with Sweet Cove from spending so much time here as a little girl, it was hard leaving my sisters, living alone, and running a new business."

Lisa didn't say anything.

Angie continued, "It can be hard to deal with life stresses. They can take a toll."

Lisa was looking out the window at the ocean. "Yes, they can."

Sitting across from Lisa put Angie in a state of discomfort. The woman would barely converse and her mood was so morose that it caused Angie's stomach to tighten from anxiety. Looking at Lisa, a slight sensation of dizziness washed over Angie and she had to fight the urge to get up and get away from the older woman sitting across from her. This is going to be a long meal.

The waiter came over and took their orders. Angie requested another iced tea.

Since there wasn't going to be much conversation coming from Lisa, and even though she was dreading it, Angie thought she may as well bring up the subject she wanted to speak to Lisa about. She had spent hours trying to think of a sensitive way to ease into the discussion, but nothing ever seemed like a good way to do it. She took a deep breath.

"I wanted to bring something up," Angie started.

Lisa's eyes grew wide and her hand fluttered as she reached for her glass.

"It's about the day the professor died." Angie leaned forward and kept her voice low. "I've been thinking about it, going over the day in my head."

The older woman stared at Angie.

"I think I saw something," Angie said.

The color drained from Lisa's face. She gripped her water glass so tightly that Angie was afraid it would shatter in her hand. "Like what?" Lisa's voice shook.

"Well, I'm not sure, but I wonder if I saw something...."

"What do you mean?" Lisa looked like she might jump out of her skin.

"I could be wrong. It was busy that day. I could be interpreting things wrong." Angie didn't want to say too much. She hoped that Lisa might offer some tidbit of information about what she saw that day.

Lisa shifted in her chair. "What? What do you think you saw?"

Ugh. Why can't she say something about that day? This is going nowhere. Angie's heartbeat was hammering. She wasn't sure how to proceed since she really didn't see anything at all that day and she didn't want to make up something in case it didn't jibe with what Lisa might have seen.

"I don't want to accuse anyone." Angie thought that comment was safe. "I just wondered...."

Lisa rubbed her throat. When she spoke, her voice was hoarse. "What are you saying? What did you see?"

Angie whispered, "I might have seen someone put something into the professor's drink."

"Who? Who did you see do it?"

"I'm not ready to accuse anyone. I'd like to hear what you have to say about the day."

Lisa jumped up from the table. "I can't talk about this. I'm getting out of here." She grabbed her purse and whirled for the exit.

"Lisa!" Angie stood up, surprised at Lisa's extreme reaction. The other patrons in the restaurant gawked at Lisa as she stormed away and then they turned their gaze onto Angie.

Angie sat down, flustered and upset, about to burst into tears. After a few minutes of trying to slow her breathing and looking out the window at the dark ocean, the tension in her body started to ease slightly and she regained her composure. Her hands were still shaking when the waiter approached the table. Angie looked up. "I'm sorry. My friend got some disturbing news," she lied. "She had to leave. Is it too late to cancel our orders?"

The waiter said, "That's completely understandable. The dinners are almost finished. Why don't I pack them up to take with you?"

Angie nodded. "Thank you. I apologize."

"No need." The waiter headed to the kitchen.

Angie took out her phone and texted Jenna. It was a disaster. I'll call you soon.

The waiter returned with the dinners in boxes and Angie carried them outside, being sure not to make eye contact with anyone in the restaurant as she hurried to leave. Stepping into the cool night air, Angie shivered but was grateful for the refreshing breeze and was glad to be out of the restaurant. On the way to her car, that internal humming vibrated through her blood again, but this time it didn't disturb Angie. It almost felt comforting. A sense of power and strength flooded through her muscles.

Angie did an about-face and headed away from the parking lot. She walked a few feet across the resort's lawn and stopped. For a full minute, she stared through the darkness to the spot where her grandmother's cottage once stood, feeling the thrumming moving through her body. Angie closed her eyes for several seconds and an idea fluttered through her mind. When she opened her eyes, the faintest smile played at the edges of her lips, and she raised her face to the yellow sliver of moon in the black sky. I'm on the wrong track, aren't I?

20

When Angie returned home and opened the front door of the Victorian, Euclid was sitting on the floor of the foyer waiting for her. Angie bent to pat the orange cat's cheeks and he turned his head from side to side to be sure that each cheek would receive several rounds of scratching.

"What a good boy. You were waiting for me to get home?"

Angie kicked off her shoes, and she and Euclid headed down the hall to the kitchen. She filled the kettle and placed it on the burner, then opened the cabinet and retrieved a kitty treat. Euclid accepted the treat and rubbed around Angie's legs, purring.

"It was quite an evening, Euclid. Lisa stormed

out of the restaurant when I brought up the day of Professor Linden's murder." Euclid stopped purring. "I know I'm thinking about this wrong. I can feel the answer pricking at the back of my mind but I just can't see it clearly."

Angie poured her tea and lifted her cell phone. "I need to call Jenna and Ellie to tell them what happened." Euclid jumped up to his perch on top of the refrigerator.

"Hey, Jenna."

Jenna put her phone on speaker so Ellie could hear as Angie relayed the whole story of her dinner with Lisa.

"That's really disappointing," Ellie said. "I was sure she'd spill what she saw."

"She is super freaked out," Jenna said. "She must be terrified that killer is going to come after her."

Angie said, "Something feels off. I think we're thinking about this wrong."

"How do you mean?" Ellie asked. "Like what?"

"When I stood outside the resort, I had a funny feeling, and then all of a sudden I knew I was going about this wrong. It was like a split second of clarity, and then it slipped away. I need to keep thinking about it. I feel like the answer is right in front of us."

Jenna said, "We need to talk to Chief Martin and

tell him our thoughts about Betty and her poisonous plants. We should tell him we think Lisa knows something, or saw something. He better talk to her before she leaves Sweet Cove."

"If he doesn't come in to the bake shop tomorrow, let's go see him at the police station." Angie took a sip of her tea.

"We're going to do a little more shopping and then stop for something to eat before we come back. We'll be home by 11pm," Ellie said.

"Okay. Don't hurry. Have a nice time. I'm going to make a fire and sit with Euclid. I need to give my mind a rest." They clicked off.

Angie went to her room and changed into yoga pants, a loose shirt, and slippers. Euclid was sticking to her like glue, following her about the house. "Are you my shadow tonight, Euclid? You're trying to make me feel better, I think. What a good boy." Angie scratched his cheeks again which set off another round of purring. "Let's get a fire going."

They went down to the first floor and into the living room where Angie prepared a fire and placed the metal screen in front of the flames. She made more tea and carried it to the coffee table. Euclid was already curled up on the sofa and Angie sat beside him. She pulled a throw blanket over her legs and the orange cat snuggled beside her. In five minutes, they were both snoozing.

THE RINGING of the front doorbell woke Angie and Euclid with a start, and the cat arched its back and growled low in his throat. Angie sat up, blinking, her heart pounding, trying to orient herself to where she was.

The bell rang again.

"The girls must have forgotten their keys," Angie told the cat. She rubbed her eyes to fully wake up. She crossed the foyer with Euclid next to her and opened the door.

"You forgot your key?" she teased before seeing who was standing there on the porch. "Oh." Angie's eyes widened with surprise.

Lisa Barrows stood on the front porch, her face serious, her brow creased from worry. "Can I come in?"

Angie stepped back so Lisa could enter. Euclid darted to the bottom stair of the curved staircase and let out a growl.

"I want to talk. I'm sorry I ran out on you like that earlier." Lisa's short salt and pepper hair was mussed like she had just gotten out of bed and dark circles under her eyes stood out prominently against her pale skin.

"Sure. It's okay. I know things have been hard for you lately." Angie lifted her hand and gestured towards the living room. "I was just enjoying the fire. Why don't we sit?"

Lisa walked with Angie into the living room. Lisa sat down on the sofa and Angie took a seat next to her. Euclid stood in the entrance of the living room staring at the women. He let out a howl. Angie and Lisa jumped at the cat's screech.

"Stop that, Euclid," Angie told the cat. She looked at Lisa. "He gets like this sometimes."

Lisa was wringing her hands in her lap. Her eyes darted about the room. "Where are your sisters? Do they want to sit with us?"

"Courtney is still in Boston finishing up school. She'll be done soon and then she'll move up here with us. Ellie and Jenna are out." Angie waited to hear why Lisa came to see her and what she wanted to talk about.

Lisa glanced at Angie's half full mug.

"Oh, would you like some tea or coffee?" Angie asked.

"If you wouldn't mind?" Lisa said. "I'm feeling a

little cold. Tea would be nice." She tried to smile, but it ended up looking like a slight grimace.

"I'll be right back. It'll only take a minute." Angie stood up.

"Can I help?"

"No. Just sit and enjoy the fire."

Euclid sat like a stone at the edge of the living room, his eyes trained on Lisa. In a few minutes, Angie returned carrying a tray. There was a ceramic teapot on it, along with a mug, a small wicker box with different kinds of tea bags in it, a silver bowl of sugar cubes, silver tongs, a spoon, and a porcelain creamer. "Here we are. I wasn't sure what kind of tea you liked so I brought a few different ones to choose from."

"Thank you so much." Lisa leaned towards the tray.

Euclid arched his back and hissed. Lisa's hand froze in mid-air as she was reaching for a tea bag.

"Euclid, stop, or I'll put you in the kitchen. He acts fussy sometimes when new people come to the house." Angie lifted the tea pot and filled Lisa's mug, then she topped off her own cup.

"I'm sorry our chat this evening upset you," Angie told the older woman. Angie didn't know why, but her heart was pounding and her muscles felt tight. She wished Lisa had called first before just showing up on the doorstep. The beginning of a headache pulsed at Angie's temples.

Lisa added cream to her tea and lifted the cup to her lips. "It's because the murder has me shook up. I haven't gotten over my mother's passing, and then all this happens on top of that."

"I understand." Angie had a slight sensation of dizziness again and that darn internal thrumming started moving through her veins. Angie rubbed her forehead. *That stupid humming has never happened to me away from the point. What's going on?*

Lisa said something but Angie didn't quite hear it. "What?"

"The tea's really good."

Angie looked at Lisa and a terrible chill ran down her spine. *What's wrong with me?* Her hand shaking, she reached for her tea mug and lifted it to her lips.

Euclid shot off his haunches like a heat seeking missile and launched over the coffee table, smashing into Angie's hand and knocking the mug of tea to the floor.

"Euclid!" Angie bolted to standing position about to chastise the cat, but then, the same sense of strength she felt outside the resort earlier in the evening flowed through her body. Her blood turned cold like some evil thing had taken hold of her.

Angie slowly turned to Lisa and their eyes met.

"You." The word fell like a boulder from Angie's lips. "It was you all along." Her voice dripped with disgust. She glanced at her mug lying on the carpet. "You put poison in my tea."

Lisa lunged at Angie and grabbed her around the throat. The force of the attack knocked both of them to the floor. Euclid leaped onto Lisa's back, stabbed his claws into her skin and bit at her neck. Euclid's vicious assault caused Lisa's grip on Angie's neck to loosen for a moment, and Angie shoved her hand under the woman's jaw and snapped her head back. Angie rolled to the side and sprang to her feet. She grabbed the teapot filled with hot water. Euclid hurtled away from Lisa and Angie flung the hot water into her attacker's face. Lisa's shrieks assaulted Angie's eardrums.

Angie ran to the fireplace and snatched up the fireplace poker. She held it out in front of her like a lance.

Lisa scrambled to her feet and dashed wildly through the foyer to the front door with Angie and Euclid chasing her. Just as she reached for the knob, the door opened. Lisa crashed past Jenna and nearly knocked her to the floor.

"Stop her! Angie called to Ellie who was on the walkway carrying shopping bags towards the porch.

Ellie dropped the bags and tackled Lisa as she tried to run past. Angie and Euclid dashed down the porch steps to where Lisa and Ellie had landed in the grass. Ellie jumped up as Lisa rolled onto her back. Her eyes widened when she saw Angie standing over her brandishing the fireplace poker at her throat.

"Don't think I won't use it," Angie growled.

Euclid, right by Angie's side, hissed menacingly at the woman on the ground.

Jenna stood on the porch with her hands on her hips gaping at the scene before her. "I guess it's time to call 911."

21

"**E**uclid knew all along," Angie said. "I should have paid more attention to him."

"I'm not sure the cat knew from the beginning, but he probably sensed something about your tea." Jenna sat down on the sofa next to Angie, Euclid sitting between them.

"She was going to poison you," Ellie's voice trembled. "Just like she did to the professor.

"When I went into the kitchen to make tea for Lisa, she slipped the poison into the mug that I left on the coffee table. It was half-full."

"Euclid must have watched her do it." Courtney had come back to Sweet Cove as soon as she heard what happened to Angie. She focused her attention to Euclid. "You are such a good cat."

Euclid puffed himself up at Courtney's praising tone.

Jenna asked, "When did you know Lisa was the killer?"

"I was feeling odd when she showed up at the door. I had that same strange feeling that I always have when I'm on the point."

Courtney was on the floor eating a bowl of cereal. She didn't look up. "Yeah, I know that feeling."

Angie's jaw dropped. The three sisters stared at Courtney as she reached for a napkin on the coffee table. She noticed the girls looking at her. "What?"

"You have a strange feeling when you're on the point?" Angie asked.

Courtney nodded. "It's not strange. It's nice." She wiped a bit of milk off her chin.

"Why didn't you ever say anything about it before?" Jenna asked.

Courtney shrugged. "I thought it was normal. I thought we all felt it."

"What do you feel?" Angie's blue eyes were like lasers on her sister.

Courtney put another spoonful of cereal into her mouth and answered while she chewed. "You know. Like my body is humming inside, just a little bit."

She put the bowl to her lips and tipped it to pour the milk into her mouth.

"Nice manners." Ellie scowled.

"It's only you three. I wouldn't do this in front of anyone else." Courtney placed her empty bowl on the coffee table. Euclid stepped onto the table and put his face into the bowl to lick up any residual milk.

"So you feel humming." Angie wanted more information.

Courtney pulled her legs in close and hugged them. She placed her chin on one of her knees. Her honey colored hair fell forward over her shoulders. "Yeah. Humming. A warmth inside of me. Like something's calling to me. It makes me feel like I belong."

Angie didn't know why, but her eyes filled up with tears. She brushed them away and cleared her throat. "Doesn't it bother you? Doesn't it make you feel weird?"

Courtney had a puzzled expression on her face. "Why would it? Nana said it was normal. For us."

"When did she tell you that?" Jenna's eyes narrowed.

"I asked her about it one summer. When, I was

little. She said it would probably get stronger as we got older."

"We?" Ellie's eyes were wide. She shifted nervously in her seat.

Courtney nodded. "Yeah. All of us. Nana said some siblings feel it stronger than others. I can't believe this is news to you three."

"Why don't I feel it?" Jenna asked. She looked like she had been left out of something.

"You probably don't listen," Courtney told her matter-of-factly.

"I guess I don't listen either." Ellie pouted.

"Did Nana feel it?" Angie asked.

"Of, course. It's hereditary. But only girls inherit it."

"Mom felt it?" Jenna asked.

"Well," Courtney said, "she could have, but she didn't want to. Nana said Mom didn't like talking about it and I should just ask Nana questions."

Angie, Ellie, and Jenna both said, "Really?"

Courtney rolled her eyes. "Didn't you ever talk to Nana? Ask her stuff?"

"You're making this up," Ellie accused Courtney.

Courtney shrugged. "Think what you want." She patted Euclid who had curled up next to her, purring.

The girls sat in silence, dumbfounded. They wondered what else they didn't know.

Courtney said to Angie, "So you felt the humming and then you knew Lisa was the killer?"

Angie swallowed hard and shook her head trying to clear away her surprise over Courtney's revelations. She gazed across the room, remembering what happened. "Not really. I didn't understand why I could feel the humming since I wasn't on the point, that's where I've only ever noticed it. Lisa and I were sitting here on the sofa. I felt the humming, and my head felt kind of dizzy. I picked up my mug. That's when Euclid jumped at me. He hit my hand and I dropped the tea." She raised her eyes. "And then I knew."

"Cool. Maybe the humming will turn into special powers," Courtney said.

Ellie had a look of horror on her face. "What? Special powers?"

"Did Nana have special powers?" Jenna said softly. Her expression indicated she might be afraid of the answer.

"I asked Mom that once. She told me not to talk about it. So maybe that means yes." Courtney chuckled.

Ellie shivered and looked at Courtney like she didn't know her. "Do you have powers?"

"Not yet, but I hope I will someday." Courtney sat up and turned to Angie. "Do you?"

Angie's eyes were wide. She shook her head.

"Well, you're the oldest. If it's going to happen to any of us, I bet it will happen to you first." Courtney lifted her empty cereal bowl from the table and got up to bring it to the kitchen. She stopped and turned around. Her eyes were bright as she said to Angie, "Your baking."

Angie looked at her with a quizzical expression.

Courtney said with excitement in her voice, "When you bake, when you make the drinks. Some of the customers ask that only you make their orders. You must be able to put something special into the things you make, something magical. Maybe that's going to be one of your powers."

Angie opened her mouth to say something, but then she closed it.

The doorbell rang. "I'll get it," Courtney said.

"Now, what?" Ellie said. She looked like she couldn't take much more.

Courtney opened the door and greeted the person. "Oh, hi. Come in."

Police Chief Martin entered the foyer. He saw the

girls in the living room, smiled, and nodded. They invited him in and he took a seat in a chair next to the sofa.

"Doing okay, Angie?" he asked.

Angie smiled. "Yeah. I'm feeling much better now. Now that everything's solved."

The chief said, "Lisa Barrows confessed to the murder of Professor Linden. She's been arrested. She claimed she only wanted to make the professor sick, she said she never intended to kill her."

"Why make her sick?" Angie asked.

"She said she was tired of demanding old people." He looked over at Angie. "Lisa said the professor was rude always wanting you to make her drinks. She said Professor Linden was a pain. Lisa actually used stronger words than that but you get my meaning."

Ellie asked, "Did she use poisonous plants?"

The chief shook his head. "She used her eye drops."

Angie sat up. "What?" Her jaw dropped. She couldn't believe that eye drops could kill someone. "She always had her eye drops with her at the bake shop. She used eye drops to kill the professor?"

The chief said, "Lisa had been putting them into the professor's drinks every chance she got. We talked to the professor's doctor. Professor Linden had a heart condition. The doc said an ingredient in the eye drops would have played havoc with the professor's heart rhythm. We suspect that when the professor fell over a month ago, it was due to the eye drops that had been put in her drinks. It built up in her system, and the last time she drank the tainted coffee, it put her heart into arrhythmia and killed her."

"How terrible," Jenna whispered. She put her hand over her mouth.

"Lisa's rantings about old people got us thinking." The chief rubbed his forehead. "We talked to the authorities in the town where Lisa used to live. There's suspicion that Lisa may have murdered her mother. In the same way."

Ellie gasped.

Angie said, "So Lisa wasn't upset about her mother's passing at all. We thought Lisa was afraid that she was in danger from Professor Linden's killer, but her distress actually came from her fear of being caught." She shook her head, shocked at the news. It was hard for her to believe that the person she worked with almost every day for a year could be capable of such things.

Jenna looked at Angie. "She quit the bake shop

because you started asking questions about who the killer could be."

"She freaked when you talked to her at dinner because she was afraid that you were going to accuse her." Courtney sat back down on the floor and looked at Angie. "So she came to kill you too."

Angie flopped against the sofa back. The reality of how close she came to dying was just starting to hit her.

The doorbell rang again. Courtney chuckled. "Now, who?"

Betty Hayes, the Realtor, was at the door holding a huge glass vase full of colorful flowers. "These are for Angie."

Courtney took the vase and Betty came in. She saw everyone in the living room and rushed over, leaned down and gave Angie a hug. "You poor dear. What you've been through. But you saved the day. You discovered the murderer." She smiled broadly. "I brought you some flowers from my garden and greenhouse."

Angie thanked Betty.

"I must be off to an appointment. You take care now. I'll see you at the bake shop. Only a few more days until you close and then we'll have to wait months for your wonderful treats." Betty bustled to the door and was gone.

"That was nice of her," the chief said, admiring the flowers.

Angie gave him a pointed look. "She just wants me to sell the Victorian. She just wants the listing."

The chief groaned. "Oh. I thought she was being nice out of the goodness of her heart."

Everyone laughed.

Courtney glanced at the bouquet sitting in the middle of the coffee table. "Look. There's oleander and lily of the valley."

Ellie's eyes went wide and her face blanched. The girls smiled at their sister's reaction.

"What?" the chief asked.

"Those flowers are poisonous," Courtney told him. "We were sure Betty was the killer."

The chief laughed at that suggestion, and then his face turned serious. "Well, I guess you never really know someone, do you?"

Euclid sniffed the flowers, and just as Angie was going to scoop him away from them, he pulled his face back from the blossoms, flicked his tail, and started to walk away.

"You know, I think Euclid is smarter than all of us." Angie gave him an admiring look.

Courtney smiled. "He thinks he is anyway."

Euclid paused and turned back to Courtney, his green eyes making eye contact with her. He put his snoot in the air and exited the room.

"Well, I guess he told you," Jenna said.

Their chuckles rippled through the room.

22

It was moving day at the bake shop. Angie arrived before anyone else. She just wanted to sit there alone in the quiet for a while with the sun filtering in through the window. She was going to miss the little place, the bustle, the customer chit chat, even the early mornings. Moving to Sweet Cove was the best decision she'd ever made and she was happy to be part of the community. Her bake shop had changed her life. Soon she would be the owner of the Victorian, a house she'd always admired whenever she and her family walked by it when she was a little girl. Angie and her sisters were able to live together again and soon would be running their businesses out the house. A wave of gratitude to Professor Linden rushed over her. She still couldn't believe the professor had bequeathed the house to her, and try as she might, she just didn't understand why. Was it simply that I had been kind to her?

Angie heard the rumble of a truck pull to a stop outside next to the sidewalk. She could see Tom jump out of the passenger side as one of his buddies came around the front.

Angie stood and opened the door for them.

"All ready to go?" Tom had a big cheery grin on his face and the look of him helped to push away Angie's melancholy feelings about leaving her shop. Another truck pulled up and two men removed a couple of moving dollies from the back. Ellie's van came to a stop at the sidewalk and Angie's three sisters hopped out and entered the bake shop. They each carried a pair of work gloves.

"We're ready to get this party started." Courtney pulled her gloves on. "What's first to be moved?"

Angie laughed. She pointed to a stack of boxes near the back room. Courtney lifted one. "What do you have in here? Cement?" She lugged it to the back of Ellie's van.

Jenna gave Angie a hug. "Are you doing okay?"

Angie nodded and gave her sister a smile. "I'm ready. Even though I'll miss this place, I'm ready to move to the next stage of things. I'm nervous, but excited."

A familiar voice spoke from the doorway of the shop. "I think it's going to be great for you."

Angie turned to see Josh Williams walking into the bake shop. Her stomach did a little flip at the sight of him. She was surprised to see him dressed in jeans and a T-shirt, his broad, strong shoulders evident under the thin fabric. The look in his blue eyes made Angie's muscles go weak.

"This is a surprise." Angie ran her hand over the top of her head in a futile attempt to smooth her hair.

"A good surprise I hope." Josh walked over to Angie. "I can't very well kick you out of your shop and not expect to help you move." His smile sent warm shivers over her skin.

"I intend to blame your brother for forcing me out, not you." Angie's eyes twinkled.

"I'm glad to hear you tell your sister that you're excited for the move. I've felt badly that our business plans conflicted with yours and you have to move out." Josh's voice was warm.

"It's actually working out for the best."

"All's well that ends well, I hope." Josh leaned against the counter.

"I hope so." Angie wasn't only talking about the moving of the shop when she said that.

"Are you two gonna' yammer all day or give us a hand?" Tom winked at Angie. He and his buddies had gone in and out several times already carrying boxes and furniture while Angie made eyes at Josh.

Angie blushed and turned to pick up a box. She looked over her shoulder at Tom and kidded him. "Okay, Task Master. I'm getting to work. Remember, I'm the one who packed these boxes all by myself."

Tom chuckled and shook his head. "Boo hoo."

With all the help, the moving of the bake shop furniture, pots, pans, baking tools, dishes, and appliances was completed in a few hours. Everything was packed away and stored on the first floor of the carriage house behind the Victorian.

The day before the move the girls had made several different kinds of lasagna, one veggie, one with spicy chicken, and a third with meatballs and sausages. They carried a long table to the wraparound porch and brought out the garlic bread, salad, and lasagnas and placed it in the middle of the wooden table.

"This smells great," one of Tom's friends remarked.

"It's the least we can do for all of your help."

Angie and Ellie placed two bottles of wine, some beer, and two jugs of iced tea beside the food. "Come and sit down, everyone."

The men and women took seats around the table and dug into the hearty meal. Euclid sat on a white wicker table next to them and watched the humans devour the food. The setting sun painted the sky with pink and violet, and Jenna lit candles as dusk settled over them. Anyone who was paying attention couldn't deny the sparks that flashed across the table between Jenna and Tom, and Angie and Josh.

They spent over two hours eating and talking, and when it was time for dessert, Courtney brought out some treats that Angie had baked for the occasion, a fruit pie and a chocolate cake covered in ganache. Angie carried a third treat to the table. She'd created a cake in the shape of the Victorian and had sculpted four women who looked very much like Angie and her sisters who sat in rockers on the tiny front porch of the creation. There was even an orange cat perched on the little railing of the house. Everyone laughed and applauded the masterpiece.

After stuffing themselves further, Tom and his friends decided it was time to head out as they had an early morning on Sunday. They had fallen behind on some building projects and planned to get some work hours in tomorrow to get them back on schedule. The girls made sure that everyone left with doggie bags packed with leftovers.

Angie walked Josh to his car. "Thank you for your help today."

"I'm glad to do it." Josh opened the driver's side door of his car. "Are we still on for the bike ride tomorrow?"

"I think we're going to be sore from the moving, but, yeah, I'm looking forward to it." Angie grinned. "I might need to tie a rope to your bike so you can pull me, though."

Josh chuckled. "No problem." His eyes held Angie's. "I'm looking forward to it too."

Angie thought for a second that Josh was going to lean in and kiss her, but then he hesitated, and seemed unsure.

"Good night, Angie. See you tomorrow." Josh slid into the driver's seat and shut the door.

Angie sighed. "Good night, Josh."

She waved as the car pulled out of the driveway and turned onto Beach Street.

BACK IN THE VICTORIAN, the sisters gathered in the den. Courtney brought in bowls of popcorn.

Angie said, "I won't know what to do with myself now that the bake shop is closed."

"We have the first bed and breakfast guests arriving in less than a week," Ellie reminded her. "We've got plenty to do to keep you busy."

Angie sat down on one of the sofas. "I'm thankful that the professor's killer has been caught and we don't have to worry about who did it and what will happen next."

Jenna sat next to Angie. She placed two mugs of tea on the coffee table in front of them. "I'm still suspicious of that lawyer, though."

Ellie said, "Maybe he was in here that night just doing what he says, looking for the most recent will. Maybe he's just odd and there's nothing under-handed going on."

"He's odd all right." Courtney rolled her eyes. "There's no denying that."

Jenna scowled. "I still think he's up to something. We need to be careful of him."

"Well." Angie yawned, tired from the busy day of moving. "Maybe that's a mystery for another day."

Euclid leaped onto her lap and started to purr as Angie scratched him under his chin. Courtney clicked the television on and started the movie. The sisters snuggled together on the sofas with cups of tea and blankets over their laps, comfy and cozy in their new home, and happy to be in each other's company.

THANK YOU FOR READING!

Books by J.A. WHITING can be found here:
www.amazon.com/author/jawhiting

To hear about new books and book sales, please sign
up for my mailing list at:
www.jawhiting.com

Your email will never be sold, shared, or spammed.

If you enjoyed the book, please consider leaving a
review. A few words are all that's needed. It would be
very much appreciated.

SOME RECIPES FROM THE SWEET
DREAMS BAKE SHOP

ANGIE'S ALMOND CAKE

INGREDIENTS

Butter for the pan

6 tablespoons unsalted butter

1⅓ cups of almond meal or finely ground almonds

1 cup of granulated sugar

⅓ cup of flour

⅛ teaspoon salt

4 egg whites

1 teaspoon vanilla extract

Confectioner's sugar (to sprinkle over the top)

DIRECTIONS

Set the oven to 350 degrees.

Butter a 9-inch spring-form pan; line the

bottom with a round of parchment paper cut to fit and butter the paper.

In a saucepan over medium heat, melt the butter. Let the butter bubble (swirling the pan occasionally) for 3 minutes or until the butter turns brown and smells nutty.

<u>Quickly remove the pan from the heat to prevent burning; let cool.</u>

In a bowl, whisk the almond meal, granulated sugar, flour, and salt.

Use a rubber spatula to stir the egg whites into the almond mixture – just until blended. Add the vanilla. Slowly pour the butter into the almond mixture. Stir until blended.

Pour the batter into the pan and smooth the top.

Bake for 30 – 35 minutes or until the top is golden and a skewer or toothpick inserted into the center of the cake comes out clean.

Cool on a wire rack for 10 minutes. Run a knife around the edge of the cake and unlatch the sides of the pan.

Use a wide metal spatula to transfer the cake to a platter or a cake stand.

Sprinkle with confectioner's sugar.

ANGIE'S GIANT CHOCOLATE CHIP SCONE

INGREDIENTS

2 cups of flour

2 teaspoons baking powder

¼ teaspoon salt

3 tablespoons sugar

4 tablespoons (½ stick) of cold unsalted butter (cut into chunks)

7 tablespoons half-and-half

1 egg plus 1 extra yolk

2 teaspoons vanilla extract

1 cup of semi-sweet chocolate chips

Extra sugar to sprinkle on the top

DIRECTIONS

Set the oven to 375 degrees. Line a baking sheet with parchment paper.

In a large bowl, whisk together the flour, baking powder, salt, and the 3 tablespoons sugar – just to blend them.

Scatter the chunks of butter over the flour mixture. Use a pastry blender or two blunt knives to cut the butter into the flour until it is reduced to pea-size pieces.

In a small bowl, whisk together half-and-half, egg, extra yolk, and vanilla.

Pour the egg mixture over the flour mixture and scatter the chocolate chips on top. With a rubber spatula, stir the mixture to form a dense dough. Knead it lightly in the bowl for 5-7 turns.

Form the dough into a plump ball about 4-5 inches in diameter.

Lift the ball onto the baking sheet.

Use a sharp paring knife to slash a shallow "X" in the top.

Sprinkle extra sugar over the top.

Bake for about 40 minutes or until it sets and turns golden brown.

Transfer to a wire rack and cool.

Use a serrated knife to cut it into wedges.

ANGIE'S PEAR FRANGIPANE TART

Choose pears that are firm but ripe as overripe
pears will fall apart during the baking.
Use a 9-inch tart pan with removable base.

INGREDIENTS FOR THE CRUST

½ cup (one stick) unsalted butter (room
temperature)

¼ cup sugar

1 egg yolk

1 tablespoon heavy cream

1½ cups flour

⅛ teaspoon salt

DIRECTIONS FOR THE CRUST

Cream the butter and sugar until soft and light.

Add the egg yolk and when the mixture is smooth, beat in the cream.

Use a rubber spatula to scrape down the sides of the bowl.

Add the flour and salt.

Mix until the dough forms large moist clumps (you don't want a ball).

Turn the clumps onto a floured counter. Shape the dough into a flat disk and wrap it in foil. Refrigerate for 30 minutes.

On a lightly floured counter, roll the dough into a 10-inch round.

Lift the pastry onto the rolling pin and lay it on the tart pan. Ease the dough into the pan, pressing it firmly into the edges. Roll the pin over the top of the pan to cut off excess dough. Refrigerate for 30 minutes.

INGREDIENTS FOR THE FRANGIPANE

4 tablespoons (½ stick) unsalted butter (room temperature)

¼ cup sugar

1 egg

⅓ cup ground almonds

1 tablespoon flour

Pinch of salt

DIRECTIONS FOR THE FRANGIPANE

Cream the butter and sugar until soft and light.

Add the egg and mix well.

Using a rubber spatula, scrape down the sides of the bowl.

Beat in the flour, almonds, and salt.

INGREDIENTS FOR THE FILLING

4 ripe Bosc pears, peeled, cored and thinly sliced

2 tablespoons apricot jam

1 teaspoon water

DIRECTIONS FOR THE FILLING

Set the over to 375 degrees.

Use a rubber spatula to spread the frangipane evenly in the pastry.

Arrange the pear slices, overlapping, pointing the narrow ends towards the center.

Press the slices lightly into the frangipane.

Bake for 50-60 minutes. Halfway through baking, rotate the pan front to back.

The filling will be firm and golden; if the edges brown too quickly while baking, cover the edges with foil.

Remove the tart from the oven and place on a wire rack. Cool completely.

In a small sauce pan, combine apricot jam and water.

Stir over high heat for 1-2 minutes or until jam loosens.

Use a pastry brush to brush the top of the tart with the glaze.

ANGIE'S HOT FUDGE SAUCE

Takes 1-2 minutes to make

INGREDIENTS

Blend the following:

1 cup of sugar

2 Tablespoons flour

½ cup cocoa

½ teaspoon salt

DIRECTIONS

Transfer to a saucepan.

Add 1 cup of boiling water and 1 tablespoon butter.

Cook over medium heat stirring constantly until thick; remove from burner.

Add 1 teaspoon vanilla extract.

ANGIE'S RUSSIAN TEACAKE COOKIES

INGREDIENTS

- 1 cup of soft butter
- ½ cup powdered sugar
- 2 cups flour
- 2 teaspoons vanilla extract
- ¼ teaspoon salt
- 2 cups of finely chopped walnuts

DIRECTIONS

Gradually add powdered sugar to butter and cream thoroughly.

Add vanilla.

Add flour, salt, and walnuts.

Blend well and chill for 1-2 hours in the refrigerator.

Shape into 1 inch balls.

Place on a greased cookie sheet.

Bake at 300 degrees for 25-30 minutes.

Roll in powdered sugar once while hot and then again when the cookies are cool.

Makes about 45 cookies.

ANGIE'S VEGETARIAN CHILI

<u>INGREDIENTS</u>

1 cup chopped onion (about 1 medium sized onion)

3 medium carrots, finely chopped

1 teaspoon olive oil

2 cloves of garlic, minced

½ red bell pepper, coarsely chopped

½ green bell pepper, coarsely chopped

½ jalapeno pepper, finely chopped

1 15-ounce can kidney beans, drained

1 15-ounce can black beans, drained

1-2 teaspoons chili powder, depending on taste

2 teaspoons ground cumin

½ teaspoon salt

1 28-ounce can tomatoes, crushed and slightly drained

4 tablespoons water

4 ounces low-fat shredded Cheddar cheese

DIRECTIONS

In a 2-3 quart microwave container, combine onion, carrots, oil, garlic, peppers and cover.

Cook on high for 6-10 minutes or until vegetables are softened. Stir once or twice.

Add beans, chili powder, cumin, salt, tomatoes, and water. Mix well, cover and cook on high for 10 minutes.

Top with cheese.

ALSO BY J.A. WHITING

OLIVIA MILLER MYSTERIES (not cozy)

SWEET COVE COZY MYSTERIES

LIN COFFIN COZY MYSTERIES

CLAIRE ROLLINS COZY MYSTERIES

PAXTON PARK COZY MYSTERIES

SEEING COLORS MYSTERIES

ABOUT THE AUTHOR

J.A. Whiting lives with her family in New England. Whiting loves reading and writing mystery stories.

Visit me at:
   www.jawhiting.com
   www.bookbub.com/authors/j-a-whiting
   www.amazon.com/author/jawhiting
   www.facebook.com/jawhitingauthor